# DIVINE CHILD

DESIGN & LAYOUT Nikša Eršek
PUBLISHED BY Sandorf Passage
South Portland, Maine, United States
IMPRINT OF Sandorf
Severinska 30, Zagreb, Croatia
sandorfpassage.org
PRINTED BY Znanje, Zagreb
Originally published by Fraktura as *Božanska dječica*.
Cover Image: detail from Max Pollak engraving "Maria Ley,"
courtesy of Jerome Robbins Dance Division,
New York Public Library Digital Collections.

Sandorf Passage books are available to the
trade through Independent Publishers Group:
ipgbook.com | (800) 888-4741.

National and University Library Zagreb
Control Number: 001099903

Library of Congress Control Number:
2021934653

ISBN 978-9-53351-323-2

The European Commission support for the
production of this publication does not constitute
an endorsement of the contents which reflects the
views only of the authors, and the Commission
cannot be held responsible for any use which may
be made of the information contained therein.

This Book is published with financial support by
the Republic of Croatia's Ministry of Culture and Media.

# DIVINE CHILD

TRANSLATED BY WILL FIRTH

## TATJANA GROMAČA

SAN-
DORF
PAS-
SAGE

SOUTH PORTLAND | MAINE

*Note on the pronunciation of names*

We have maintained the original spelling of proper nouns. The vowels are pronounced as in Italian. The consonants are pronounced as follows:

c = ts, as in *bits*
č = ch
ć = similar to č, like the t in *future*
dž = g, as in g*eneral*
đ = similar to dž
j = y, as in y*ellow*
r = trilled as in Scottish; sometimes used as a vowel, e.g. "Krk," roughly "Kirk"
š = sh
ž = like the s in *pleasure*

# Contents

*For Radenko and Marta*

"Ah, these centuries, history's favorite unit, relieving the individual of the necessity of personally evaluating the past, and awarding him the honorable status of victim of history."

JOSEPH BRODSKY *Flight from Byzantium*

# PART I

*A general introduction to Mother's world,*
*her personal illness, and that of the wider society.*

*Lies and theft vs. freedom and authenticity*

THOSE WHO RULED the country lied and stole without anyone punishing them for their "work," although there were witnesses and evidence of their lies and theft, lying and thievery were indirectly legalized, so everyone whose conscience permitted it was able, and encouraged, to lie and steal. As such, they were valuable and useful to society because they acted in accordance with the most shining examples, and they were also at the top, so it was clear that only those high up could get away with wholesale lying, theft, and raking in the wealth of others, taking from everyone, who were fools because they allowed others to lie to them and steal from them.

The lowest were not the illiterate, whose illiteracy and ignorance made them support those who lie and steal because they were impressed by their haughtiness and arrogance and thought it was proof of their greatness and importance. The lowest in society were those who believed in ideals and still fought for ideals—loyalty, goodness, truth, integrity, love, sincerity, reliability, trust—in a way that others considered good, upright, and considerate.

Deep inside, everyone believed others could defraud them, unless they were naïve fools from the bottom of the pyramid who took the ideals literally, and no one knew yet if they stole and lied. In fact, most people knew that others stole and lied, and not only that, but they knew exactly who stole what, who they lied to and when, but they pretended not to know. That knowledge connected them in a chain, as it were, in which everyone stood holding others by the reins, whose secret lying and stealing they knew about. In that way, no one was completely free to exempt themselves from the chain in which they stood, but that lack of freedom and authenticity was justified by the realization that others were not entirely free or authentic either, believing that one could not be completely free and authentic.

If there did really exist people who were entirely free and authentic in their thoughts and actions, or who strove for that in their life and thoughts, they were removed in a peaceful way like crushed bugs that are swept under the rug, where they managed to linger on, taking short breaths through moth holes in the frayed weaves, but only enough that they not wither up entirely.

There were many such people who deep inside wished to be free and authentic but believed it was not yet totally and completely possible, or who believed it was simply necessary to adapt to the lack of freedom and authenticity in order to remain on the surface and so as not to be swept under the rug. They had good adaptation skills and were equally convincing actors, traits they used to assure themselves and others that they had never been interested in being free and authentic for an instant, while at the same time believing deep inside that freedom and authenticity were things that inspired them the most of all and made their chests swell, and they were glad, if nothing else, about others' courage to be free and authentic.

I reflected on that as the watchman sitting in his box at the entrance to the hospital grounds raised the boom barrier. It was sufficient to wave to him from the car, and he already knew who we were and whom we were coming to see. He would always wave back as if we were friends, and it seemed we were in a way, and that we understood everything about one another without exchanging a single word.

We understood the watchman and how it was for him to sit in the box there in winter above the glowing strip of warmth emitted by the small electric fan heater to warm his outstretched feet in thick woolen socks that one of the hospital's patients had knitted for him.

We understood the creased newspaper on the wooden table scored by knife and pen, just as we understood the pervasive smell of salami and cheese from the sandwich he was meant to eat for lunch but ate early in the morning out of boredom and impatience.

Likewise, it was completely understandable for us that the watchman in his box, who raised the barrier for the cars and ambulances at the entrance to the enormous hospital complex, which was once the sprawling estate of great counts and landowners, mostly watched TV during his long shift, on a small set fitted between two plywood shelves and the light switch on the wall.

The watchman was sleepy because he was eternally stupefied by the vacuous images he absorbed from the TV screen, but he could never muster the strength to switch it off. Besides, the worst could only come after switching it off, when faced with the question: *What now?*

And yet, the hypnosis of the screen did not cloud and lull his mind all that much. The watchman could see and understand our pain when we came to visit Mother. He was able to focus on gauging whether our pain was greater when we entered the hospital grounds or when we left, but ultimately he could hardly be sure of the constancy of the proportions he gauged.

*What is reality, and what not*
*(a link to Charles Perrault and fairy tales,*
*and to many kinds of doubts and adaptations)*

THERE WAS A peaceful and pleasant time when no one could yet imagine anything nearly as baleful, black, unbelievable, entirely unnatural, dreadful, insane, sick, beastly, and depraved, as later actually took place, when people turned into wild animals overnight and started spilling each other's entrails and devouring their organs, burning their houses, and raping women, their husbands, children, and old people, which all together was wilder than the most bloodthirsty of animals. During that still entirely innocent, complacent, and peaceful peace, when she got especially angry and flew into a rage for no particular reason—things which people generally get angry and fly into a rage about—Mother had the habit of yelling: "You'll drive me to the madhouse!"

That was her favorite phrase, which came true in the end, like the innkeeper's wife's exclamation in the fairy tale about the sausage that would grow out of her nose. In the end, or actually before the end, Mother ended up in the madhouse. And through that firsthand experience, all of us, Mother included, convinced ourselves that a madhouse was also a fairly normal place, and that there were often people in it who were a lot healthier and more normal than many of those "outside" in so-called freedom, and especially those "outside" in freedom who are considered people of importance, reputation, and power.

Mother, for example, was completely healthy and normal apart from being disturbed, and she was disturbed for entirely different, unfathomable reasons, which none of the people who should have tried to fathom actually ever did because no one really wanted to come to terms with Mother's fate and sympathize with her. In any case, Mother's faculty of judgment was normal, except that, on account of being normal, it clashed completely with the outside world, so that in a way it became unbearable for her to live in that world and interact with others since she was "too normal," which to a degree bordered on the abnormal.

All of a sudden everything went through a warp, all reality and all truth became different, and in line with that people changed too, of course, because they were forced to adjust. Sometimes the adjustment went so far that they completely negated themselves, deleting their own past, name, origin, and occupation if they were not in step with the new course in every respect.

But it was actually sufficient to pretend that one thought and lived in step with the new course, and it was not necessary to truly think and live in step with it, just as it was not at all necessary to change one's name if one lived and behaved entirely in step with the new course and did everything in order to constantly affirm from moment to moment, second to second, with all the gestures of one's existence, that one lived in step with it. One had to constantly dispel every slightest suspicion that one perhaps did not live, breathe, sleep, and dream completely in step with the new course in every living second, so people's gestures, words, and actions played a role, as did possible grimaces and ways of blowing one's nose and covering one's mouth when sneezing.

There could be all sorts of different suspicions, but undoubtedly the worst that could fall on someone was that they were of *Eastern origin*. Whether that possibly had some deep genesis and connection with *original sin* seems not yet to have been fully examined, but in any case a whiff of an Eastern origin in the new reality largely purged of Eastern origin could be smelled a mile away.

It was sufficient just to read a person's name that embodied the suspicion of possible nefarious roots for all the worst premonitions to arise and become attached to it, because an Eastern origin by itself suggested that.

But if someone invested as much effort as mentioned to *efface* their Eastern origin in the eyes of the collective Other in all possible, less possible, and yet likely ways, and if they constantly and wholeheartedly tried to prove that they had no living or nonliving connection with any Eastern origin, and that they, moreover, on account of the particular shame they felt because of it, had never traveled anywhere in the East, not even as part of the most innocuous school excursion, they could be accepted in the new reality.

Mother's problem was that she tried as hard as she could to adjust to the new reality, but equally she did not wish to erase her Eastern origin, in view of the fact that it was hers and she could equally have been born in the west, south, or north by another stroke of chance, and considering it was ridiculous, of course, to demand or expect anything of anyone, and particularly ridiculous, as well as deplorable, to demand that someone erase and completely negate part or all of themselves, in other words of that which befell them in this life by luck or sheer chance, beginning with their name or the family they were born into, and anything else.

In any case, Mother had a strange illness, which especially sensitive people suffered from. Sometimes it made her overly happy, other times endlessly sad. Sometimes when she was overly happy she would walk along the street loudly singing songs she particularly liked, for example "When the Girls Went Down to the Water" or "The Young Mowers from the Hills." Mother had a wonderful voice and a good ear. As a young woman she was a dancer of folk dances and a singer of folk songs. She wore traditional dress, which she changed into and out of depending which region the songs and dances she performed were from. She often had a flower in her hair unless, as part of the costume she had to wear a kerchief with tiny dangling ducats, a turban, a fez, or thick, woolen headscarves with colorful appliquéd flowers, which often made her head sweat profusely.

Mother's singing and dancing continued later, too, and she excelled at singing and accentuating her voice at weddings and other celebrations, and later still, when the country her father helped create fell apart and when great wars began again, with killings, rape, arson, torture, and massacres, Mother switched to the church choir so as to be closer to God by singing hymns, to pray for peace and the souls of the dead and fallen, and as such she used the beauty of her voice in a way for purposes that could be called socially useful and charitable.

ON THE OTHER hand, Mother's illness also had its other, extreme opposite, when she no longer felt at all like singing songs, celebrating life, and spreading love. Rather, entirely the opposite of excessive happiness, she would sink to the very bottom of the double bed and sleep there from morning till night, and so on without end. Those were periods when Mother turned into a sleeping beauty, sleeping a sleep so deep that no one could wake her. It looked very much as if that sleep would last for centuries, except for the fact that Mother did not resemble a beauty during that sleep. It was as if she really did not want to be beautiful at all, nor did she want anyone to love her, or she believed that she did not deserve to be loved.

She never spoke about that later when she finally emerged from her sleep, and she would not remember even a fraction of what happened during those long days of sleep. In particular, she did not remember whether she wanted anyone to love her, or whether she considered she did not deserve love, just as she did not remember that she had not washed or bathed during the long days of sleep, nor cut her nails or hair, changed her nightgown or the bed linen, nor wanted to wake up at all, no matter which prince appeared by her bed, although it was well known that there had always only been one prince for Mother from the beginning, and, as everyone knew, that was Father.

But Father too, Mother's prince, was completely helpless during the sleeping beauty phase, such that Mother's dormancy also passed to him. It seemed as if they were both covered by a gray shroud that fell upon them like a tarpaulin, and they sank into deep slumber quite forgotten and forsaken by everyone else, there in their kingdom, a great manor, over which a mantle of notoriety fell on account of Mother's sleeping illness. Its very mention would cause other people to turn their heads like Mariolino, the inquisitive boy from the Italian cartoons, whose head would hop up and down on his shoulders every so often, and his eyes would pop and roll, and afterward he had one hell of a time sitting back down in his place, or anywhere near it.

In any case, people did not know that Mother had an illness that many of the world's greatest artists, composers, and writers suffered from, such as Ludwig van Beethoven and Georg Handel, or Robert Schumann, Edvard Munch, Virginia Woolf, and Ernest Hemingway, and Mother ranked with those illustrious figures, although she could never have dreamed that she herself was, in one respect, an artist.

*Wherever she appeared she took things into her hands*
*(Mother really was a born leader)*

NOW AND THEN in Mother's mature years, usually because lying around at home became irksome to her, and on account of the existing circumstances, it was good for her to have a change of scene and go to the hospital. Whenever she went, her stay there, and she herself, gained in importance in a way, because the very fact of a person being in a place like a hospital made something of a hero of them. No longer was she anonymously battling her demons at home.

Mother felt like a hero in the hospital, and that made itself noticeable in her behavior. Soon after arriving in the particular ward and being assigned a bed, all the other women in the same ward wanted to buy Mother a coffee from the vending machine. Some of them wanted to go for a walk around the hospital grounds specifically with her—only those, of course, who had permission to go out—and so Mother did not have enough time in the end to fully satisfy them all.

Mother spent most of her time in the hospital waiting in the corridor near the phone because someone could call for her any minute. Besides, it was crucial that someone take on the task of being a telephone operator, and Mother performed the job most devotedly, which involved her calling this or that person from room number whatever to come to the phone, considering that Mother knew the names and room numbers of all the patients by heart. It was a fitting task for her, given her character and her memory, which had always served her in an exemplary manner, and which contributed to her extraordinary memory for numbers, and when great generals and statesmen were born and died, along with other facts and figures.

From time to time, Mother was also in the habit of reading books in the hospital lounge. The news on television did not interest her particularly because it lacked an extra-temporal dimension and was overly mundane and dark, which always made it seem too boring for her. And in movies there was always shooting, or constant charging about, so Mother preferred to go back to the room, lie in bed, and reminisce about pleasant days when the sun shone warmly, the fruit was ripe and begging to be picked, and she could enjoy the sky, the flowers, and meadows.

*Why the all-encompassing political turnaround overturned everything to do with Mother and she ceased to be a popular social phenomenon*

MOTHER WOULD GO without lunch on Fridays when she was in the hospital because she could not stand the smell of fish. That was because, when she was a little girl, she lived under military discipline. Her father was an army man, who, along with the military discipline and other measures, insisted that Mother and her sisters take cod liver oil in order to be forever healthy and robust, just like the toughest soldiers from ancient Sparta.

So, Mother hated fish because the cod liver oil made her hate the smell of fish, but at the same time she loved order and discipline because they had become ingrained in her bone and fiber, so she did not find it difficult, for example, when the patients had to leave their beds at seven thirty in the evening so the nurses could air the rooms. Other elements of stringency did not bother her either, nor missing out on lunch on Fridays, although one lady made up for it by giving Mother some pieces of the cured cheese she concealed in the small drawer by the head of her bed. It was a salted, cured cow's milk cheese, which is hung in string nets to dry—the kind of cheese that Mother liked most. In return, Mother would buy cigarettes at the hospital canteen for the cheese lady because she preferred to smoke than to eat fish or cheese. Since Mother never smoked, she could not distinguish the different cigarettes that were sold at the canteen, but the lady with the cheese told her that her favorite brand was called LM.

Mother immediately memorized the name because it was quite easy to memorize, consisting of just two simple letters, nothing like all of the identification numbers, telephone numbers, zip codes, and birthdays Mother had stored away over the years, along with the long series of numbers she recorded, added, and subtracted in huge ledgers with impressive dark green wooden covers, when she worked.

Mother also bought a soap container at the canteen because she washed in the hospital more than at home, where she had a lot of soap and towels. But wash as she would, no one apart from Father would accept her the way they used to.

People once accepted her well because Mother was mostly kind. She loved to help everyone, even beggars and those whose house had burned down, or those who had collapsed on the road from being dead drunk and passersby ignored. She would go to them, lift them off the road, and help them home if they could not walk or walked with difficulty because their legs were weak and wobbly.

With those who begged for money, Mother would buy them a burek, some bread, a cake, or a poppy seed bun, and Mother knew most of the names of all those who did not need anything, so when she was out and about she always greeted everyone she met, or those who were selling things by the roadside or in street-corner kiosks, from the florist to the butcher, the key cutter and the goldsmith.

Mother greeted them all with a loud "Hello!" and then their name: Beki, Branko, Robert, or Marija, and they greeted back "Hello, Lili," since Mother's nickname was Lili, just like the

TATJANA GROMAČA

popular brand of nylon stockings that Mother most liked to wear in the time she still wore nylons and dark-colored patent leather shoes, or black ankle boots with a delicate zipper at the side.

But then the turnaround occurred, when everything was suddenly overturned and everyone became full of suspicion and fear. Everyone was eyed and scrutinized in that state of suspicion and fear, and those who were suspicious were eyed and scrutinized most of all. Almost anyone could be suspicious, particularly those who might have some connection with that dreaded Eastern origin. It all came down to that because a lot of hatred was sown among people for the needs of war, and war was needed so that those who judged it necessary could earn wads of money, piles of precious furniture and gold, and after the war lots of cheap land and heaps of cheap labor and obedient subjects, and there were rumors in some places of massive oil fields, that is masses of oil wells, which were particularly essential for war.

It was necessary to sow hatred in order that it could come to war in the first place because war needed to be begun between people who thought they were not enemies, but brothers, some of whom happened to live farther east than others. Since a degree of the old hatred had been preserved from back before the big old war between the easterners and those who were less eastern, it was not at all difficult, not in the slightest, to reignite that hatred, and it soon wrought perfect havoc and turned all suspicions and scrutiny overnight into deadly weapons, bullets, bombs, and fires, gouged-out eyes and spilled entrails.

During the turnaround, everything to do with Mother was also overturned. She was no longer the popular singer and dancer in Lili stockings, but now became a maligned murderer and hideous, bearded butcher—a wild rider from the Russian steppes, a crude Turk with a rusty scimitar, a Serb dogface from the Salonica Front.

*The origins of Eastern origins*

THERE ARE MANY different sorts of knives, but the most suitable for cutting throats in war are slightly longer ones, like hunting knives brandished to kill wild pigs. They have a broader blade and can even be curved at the tip, like the Turkish scimitars that were used for slashing during the conquests five centuries before that in which the story of Mother and our family origins takes place. They can be considered rather specialized knives, and, as we know, in the war there was no opportunity to obtain state-of-the-art equipment. People therefore made do with whatever they could find, including diver's knives for catching and killing large fish, or for cutting open, gutting, or scaling fish. If there were no knives, other tools and implements were an option: axes, saws, robust scissors, and knitting needles. For those who deserved to be killed, even the most ordinary can opener worked, and there were usually plenty of those in almost all houses and farmsteads, and can openers could also be an integral or rather accessory part of a regular, soldierly meal.

In terms of knife wounds, it seems an old woman was unsurpassed—the wife of an old friend of Mother and Father's—who the records say was stabbed a total of twenty-seven times, and, as unbelievable as it sounds, by some miracle she survived, unlike most during the great killing spree of World War ii. As is fairly well known, that massacre was followed by a lot of smaller but no less assiduous ones, of which the carnage that the wife of Mother and Father's friend survived was surely one of the more impressive, since it occurred in a place of "spiritual," or rather sacral significance, that is in a church, which in the context of the war certainly had a special, far from negligible value.

But that was nothing especially new or innovative, bearing in mind that the cold, stone spaces of churches had invited such actions and activities in centuries before, and people responded especially gladly, and quite often, in almost mathematically admeasured intervals. We can only speculate as to the reasons. In any case, there were some quite fanciful deeds here, where those less encumbered by routine and restraint built towers of human skulls, for instance, but such exploits were rare and are really not worth mentioning because they only interrupt the uninspired series of monotonous massacres during long, boring, and predictable lessons in history and geography, where history is constantly being tailored and geographic definitions likewise are constantly being made over, mostly with the aid of scattered human bones and skulls—an open-air ossuary of remains that are dug up, moved around, piled, counted, and marked, leading to more searches, findings, and exhumations.

So, no one returned Mother's greetings on the street anymore, and everyone stood mutely looking at her as she went along the first, second, and third street of the town, carrying her bags with bread, parsley, celeriac, and carrots.

Mother called out "Hello!" as usual and thought she could rouse her acquaintances from their frosty silence, but she did not receive anything in return because she did not deserve it, or rather, if she did deserve anything, then it was certainly not anything good, but bad and worse than worst, because everything had changed, and in the context of those changes it was nothing short of miraculous that Mother was still alive at all.

In any case, it was just as well for Mother that she did not recover because her illness was a trifle compared with how she could have ended as a suspicious person of Eastern origin, as, after all, many ended, but about which it is not particularly appropriate or wise to speak, or even whisper.

*In the hospital, at least, everyone could be what they really were (thief, scrounger, drunkard, or gambler)*

FORTUNATELY THERE EXISTED the hospital, where everyone could be what they were. It was like that, at least, at the hospital where Mother went roughly once a year at fairly regular intervals. It was always after days when Mother could not wake up or get out of bed, and when Father managed to drag her out of bed she would immediately be taken to the hospital, to ward number such and such and room number such and such. All the rooms in that hospital were constantly full, and whoever was able to get a bed in one of the rooms was genuinely lucky, and why Mother took some pride in returning to the hospital. Mother and Father were lucky because they almost always managed to get a bed for Mother. There were a lot of beds and a lot of women in each room, and air became scarce at night because the women did not like the windows above their heads to be opened after the nightly airing.

Mother would wake up early because she felt the air was used up, so she sat on the edge of her bed and waited for morning and the time when they were allowed to go and shower. Sometimes she was woken up by "poachers," women who snuck into the rooms and stole cookies and candies from other women's bedside cabinets. One night, a woman was caught stealing, and another pawed through the lockers in the corridor. One young woman got hold of some alcohol, and when she was drunk she smashed a window with her bare hands. It took three orderlies and four nurses to tie her down with leather straps to stop her getting away.

"The woman was from the war zone and carried those traumas inside," Mother explained on the phone. "We all have that, all of that is still inside us, and that's why we're here. Plus all that we've been through in life, even without the war. Some women suffer violence at home, one is bashed by her husband when he's back from work, and now she just lies in bed with her face to the wall and doesn't speak to anyone. Another woman was discharged from the ward and was back a few days later. She had slashed both her wrists. 'How'd you do it?' I asked. 'A kitchen knife,' she said.

"Otherwise all the women are nice, they're all kind-hearted. We sit in the room and chat in the evening. There are quite a few women from our area, and some from neighboring areas, and most of them are young, so I'm almost the oldest. It's terrible to see how many young people are ill. I've been through my share. The girls are real dears, but mainly very quiet. I strike up a conversation, and they open up.

"I usually ask them how they are, what their name is, and where they're from. I ask: Did you have a job when you were well? Are you married? Do you have children? They then gradually open up and we talk, but no one has to if they don't want to. Most of the women want to talk, and there are quite a few who you can chat with about people we know, who lived in the same town and worked in some firm there.

"The one thing I can't stand is stealing. Stealing and scrounging. There are those who are constantly scrounging for you to give them something, and there are also those who steal. That's why I lock everything away in my bedside cabinet, and I also put my nightie there because if I leave it under the pillow it could get pinched. In one hospital they stole my new outfit, and one woman stole my travel bag. Not that she didn't have one herself. It's an illness, kleptomania.

"There are those who are obsessive scroungers, and mostly they scrounge for cigarettes and coffee. I walk up and down the corridor because I don't want to put on weight here. They feed us here like in a hotel, the food has got a lot better since last time. When we had an open meeting of the ward, I stood up and said what I like here and what bothers me. They asked me how I found it at the previous hospital, so I talked about that too, and they asked who the staff were and if they might know any of them, and it turned out they know the nurse Barbara.

"I said I was sorry and didn't want to seem a tattletale, but I had to bring up the case of stealing from last night. I told it all over: I heard a rustling behind my back at three thirty and Žana taking a Honey Heart out of Malina's locker. Malina couldn't run after her because she's fat, but Azra ran, having woken up, and I also got up. And afterward I couldn't get back to sleep. Now the thief will be moved to a stricter ward, maybe to a room with bars, or maybe she'll be put in an isolation cell, who knows?

"I'm not here because I drank and gambled. You know yourself about my operation, when they took out my everything, and they didn't give me any analgesic afterward. Plus the war and all I've been through, and hey presto—my illness! What can I do? I'm glad that all of you are there for me and that your dad never forced me to get out of bed when I couldn't. Other women have their illness as well as problems at home, but I don't have any problems with you."

*What happens when a person is full of*
*excessively normal ideas*

DURING HER RECREATION time in the hospital, Mother chose to play Ludo, which here goes by the name of "Man, Don't Get Angry." She had not played it for years, although she had once loved it. Now it came back to her again by chance. The game is simple: a die is thrown and the player moves their token forward the number of spaces shown on the die. The main thing is that no one gets angry when another player lands on their token and kicks them out, it is just like one animal eats another, or a person eats a plant or animal. No one is allowed to get angry—that is the gist of the game.

That is what women have been taught from time immemorial. Women have to put up with things, and every woman puts up with a lot because there is a lot of suffering in her life that she has to endure. It is best not to try and change things but to put up with them. A woman must not show others her suffering and must not cry, she must be as hard as a rock. She has to be tough to put up with everything and bear it all with a smile and serenity, for only then will she be a proper woman worthy of admiration. A woman has to be serene and contrite, as cold as a stove with no wood in it.

Mother did not caress anyone because no one caressed her, and no one taught her that caressing and affection are good. She thought coldness and restraint were good, and softness and warmth were bad because they created weaklings, and life was about struggle and strife and too hard to be warm and soft—that is what this woman thought in her inner program about how women ought to be.

Only when we learn how and what a person wishes to be can we say we know anything about them, a wise man with a white beard once said. A woman sees life as suffering, not as pleasure and joy. For her, love vanished after the first years of marriage, and now it is only a memory for her. Physicality is not pleasure and fulfillment, but suffering and sin, and the body is a stranger. It is better to have a son than a daughter because women have a harder lot in life.

Father had a problem with acceptance, and Mother with recognition. All his life, Father felt unaccepted, and therefore all his life he wished to be accepted. Sometimes he would show that desire by pretending he did not wish to be accepted and did not want to be part of anything. That was mainly when he was young and liked to fight and argue because he had a lot of energy and testosterone.

When he grew old, he no longer cared for contention and proving himself; now he wished to hide behind someone's skirts. He wished to do all he could to become part of something, but he was unable to do enough to become part of anything. Besides, there were no skirts he could see himself in, which he could sneak behind, and which he could say suited him entirely, because he did not quite fit in anywhere, or rather he always stuck out a little in one way or another.

In that respect, Father's inclinations made him more of a scientist, but in terms of his worldview he could have been an artist, and a scientist as well, because he was an idealist, but he was tormented by his strict upbringing, which did not give him the freedom to be what he was. Father's hard upbringing made him into a man who had to be like all the others, but he was not like all the others. His hard upbringing made him a sturdy man, but he had fine bones. It made him a harsh man, but his soul was soft. It made him a dissatisfied man, but he never needed a lot to be happy.

It made him a man who strove to be part of the tribe, quite the opposite of the individual and self-effacing creative, who, despite everything his hard upbringing did to obliterate, ultimately came to the surface and baffled everyone, Father himself most of all.

In contrast to Father, Mother felt accepted most of the time, except when everyone began to reject her and turn their back on her, but that, after all, was a completely different story. It was not a problem of Mother's but a problem that others had. She was inoculated against those problems because she had the spirit of a universal person, for whom all people are equal, independent of their origin, language, or religion. Father, incidentally, thought that way too, but he had to pretend to be more straight and narrow than he was in order to be accepted in that environment, so he tried hard to hate and despise those who were not of his religion and nation, especially those of Eastern origin. Mother, of course, did not belong to them, although she was undeniably of Eastern origin, because Father could not bring himself to hate her since they shared bed and table.

That was a very sensitive issue, of course, and it put Father in a most awkward situation. He was now meant to hate and despise his own wife, which seemed almost impossible, especially because he did not hate and despise her, quite the opposite. At the same time, he could no longer be part of the majority because he had a minority that was undesirable or, at the very least, stood out. He also could not become part of the minority that Mother belonged to because he did not feel that was him.

His own tribe did not want him, he was branded, and he was given that mark because of his wife, who came from a different tribe, which she did not really belong to at all, because together with Father, and even before him, she had lived all her life belonging to his tribe.

Now they were nowhere, and they could not go anywhere. It was a typical stalemate for people who were too old to sell up and migrate with the storks and swallows to Africa because everything here where they lived was so idiotic and infinitely stupid. Besides, they did not want to admit even to themselves that everything was so stupid and sick. They pretended everything was normal, but nothing was normal, although it turned out that everyone was normal apart from Mother, who went to a hospital for the abnormal. This was not because she was abnormal but because she was excessively normal, which of course was abnormal, worthy of condemnation and contempt of the highest order, so therefore it was certainly necessary for her regularly to be removed from the environment so she would not have too much of an abnormal impact on it with her excessively abnormal ideas.

*Official report from the hospital*
*(God is always with those in hardship and who suffer)*

"HELLO, YES, HOW can I help you? Ward Number 5 here, who are you calling for?"

Mother always answered the phone that way. Like Dr. Andrey Yefimich, the hero of "Ward No. 6" by Anton Pavlovich Chekhov, she was confined to a hospital for the mentally ill, and, just like that doctor, she was healthier than most of the people in freedom, outside the hospital, who walked around as if they alone were the way one has to be.

"Most of the women here are smokers, so they go to the smoking room and sit there and smoke. It stinks of cigarettes and smoke so badly—it's ghastly. I can't bear to even go past. Today I went about the rooms with a nurse and a piece of paper and wrote down the phone numbers of the women I like so I can call them when I get home. Most of the women are here because they have problems with their husbands. That's why they go to the room to smoke, so they don't have to talk. They don't want to go to the lounge because they'd have to chat with others, everyone talks there about what's tormenting them, but they don't want to. It's better to talk than . . . you know . . . to sink into all sorts of bad thoughts.

"They feed us like in a hotel. We had tomato sauce, mashed potatoes, and a frankfurter for lunch, and for dinner there was carrot and potato stew. Tomorrow I'm on duty, I'll be by the phone all day.

"The doctor told me that if your dad dies first I'm entitled to a share of his pension. But I wouldn't want to be left alone after him, I'd rather be the first to go to the pearly gates. I'd never take my own life though, I'd never do that to you. You'd be marked afterward if I killed myself."

Each time they raised Mother from bed using drugs, she would talk like that on the phone. She had so much to tell about all that happened in Ward Number 5 every day. It seemed as if there was nothing nearly as interesting in the outside world as the goings-on in Ward Number 5, or Mother was able to tell such interesting tales that everything seemed so important and good, so it really was essential to call her in the evenings because otherwise I might miss something special. What, I asked myself from time to time, but I knew the answer. I might miss a good story, and that would be a shame because Mother was there to collect good stories and tell them to me on the phone when I rang, and I was on the other end to listen to them and write them down after she told them to me.

And so everything took on a higher and wider meaning, nothing was halted but spread and grew with the aim of acquainting as many people as possible with Mother's story and for them to become aware of the real truth about her and the world she lived in. Because everyone wishes to learn the real truth, and that desire is nothing other than the desire to become closer to God, and that God is nothing other than what is true, majestic, and noble in each of us. Thus spoke a philosopher, and I would endorse it on the spot in my capacity as Mother's certified interpreter.

TATJANA GROMAČA

Besides, I think Mother also would have endorsed that because she spent so much time with God. When no one else was at her side, when she sank so deep into her dark dreams that no one could follow her into those depths, and no one dared to either because they recognized from a safe and respectful distance how terrible that was, God was with Mother because He is always, especially with those who suffer great misfortune.

If God had not been with Mother, today we would not know the whole truth about Father, her, her illness, and the war. But we know it, and it dawns before us like a bright morning comes after a great and terrible night, which seemed it would never end. Morning breaks, a pale and tender dawn. And everything comes back—the trees, the houses, the sky, the people. Even the squirrels, which hastily gnaw at the round berries on the thorny bushes by the roadside, and the birds of colorful plumage.

*How fate forced Father, although completely innocent,*
*to become an exemplary homemaker*

IN THE EVENINGS I would reflect on Father and Mother. Mother got into bed in Ward Number 5 of the hospital. Two patients had been discharged, but new women had arrived and the bed linen had just been changed. Mother lay down and reflected on the day that had passed. She was happy because she was well and would soon be going home. She was looking forward to it, there would be pleasant days, and it would soon be Christmas. Father was happy too, although a little frozen, because the stove in the workshop did not heat very well. It had also grown old and no longer heated like it once did, and it used to heat his work space so well that he had to keep the door open when he was doing his woodwork there.

During the difficult years, that stove served him not only for heating but also for cooking on top of it. He, who had hardly even boiled eggs before, now made hearty stews, creamy soups, and casseroles. He was always talking about recipes, what he was going to cook the next day, and what he and Mother now liked to eat. He had no choice, because Mother slept constantly, or more or less constantly; she only got up to eat. All the order, all the stringency of her formerly organized and disciplined life was gone. Roles suddenly became variable, hard molds cracked and crumbled into tiny pebbles. Everything became distensible and permeable, and what was once terribly important now became insignificant. Difficulties existed in order to be lessons for us, but the new knowledge could only be gained through effort and pain.

*Mother and her famous charitable streak*

MOTHER WAS REPRIMANDED in the ward. She had taken too much into her own hands, they said. She had tried to organize a collection, which she called "A kuna from everyone to buy a rose for the birthday girl." In the end, she became very sad, twice wounded. She was hurt by the women in the ward because not one of them wanted to support her drive. They all came up with the same excuse: that they did not have a single kuna on them. They turned their backs, and precisely those who had been amicable and smiling the day before suddenly became cold and distant.

"They don't care, although the woman whose birthday it was brought cakes for everyone," Mother said

But what hurt Mother most was the reprimand from the nurses. She had to submit to their will and admit that her wish to collect money for a rose was a transgression, and she was made to feel as if she deserved to be punished, although she had not done anything wrong.

"We've lived with others in humanity and kindness all our lives, but that's gone now," Mother said. "There's no warmth, neither between the women nor the nurses. There are nurses who holler around and are bossy. They have the power here and have to be obeyed. I don't like that."

Father respected the authorities in a slightly strange, not overly consistent way. On the one hand he despised and constantly criticized them, but on the other hand he needed them in order to feel secure. He thought the smartly signed official papers with a purple stamp at the bottom were a symbol of the state's concern and a guarantee of security. He liked it when a public official occasionally dropped in and would be his guest: a person with papers in their bag, who asked him to fill in his particulars—year and place of birth, education, etc. He thought the official was part of a broad, communal entity that watched over everyone and did not permit anything bad to happen, although behind the mask of general welfare many bad things did happen that did not lead to prosperity, but to dissolution, hostility, and death.

And yet the dapper impression of the attentive and serious public official with a new ballpoint pen that left no blotches on the white paper was so strong that it overlaid all other experiences and memories, and that really was a very good thing.

"There are all sorts of people, and when a lot of people come together in one place they mix and a lot of things happen, and least of all good," Mother said. "And you can't help to make things turn out for the best if others don't want to support you. You have to withdraw, and that's it. You have to accept that's the way things are, because no one wants to talk about what really torments them."

Mother was not normally so morbid. But they'd lowered her mood with drugs because she had "gone over the top" with her kunas and rose initiative. Therefore the dear, nice, and likeable women turned overnight into cold, clammy walls. Her enthusiasm for all things to come gave way to resignation, and comfort and amenity gave way to severity and punishment.

It all depended on what came from within. When things were alright inside, the outside world could be just as bad or hard, but it did not seem that way. That is the truth. But it is also true that no one wants to talk, not only about what torments them but also about the nice things. Mother was right: no one wants to talk. Everyone just wants to exert their will and expects others to go along with it unconditionally, through guilt and fear. They do not even want to talk about what they want to happen. They want it to be done exactly their way, aided by fear of punishment and a feeling of guilt, because too little of what they want ever comes to pass.

"One woman wanted to kill her husband. She stabbed him several times. She went to jail for four years, and now she's here for treatment. I wouldn't dare to stab your dad. Just think what he'd do to me if I stabbed him. He'd take the knife and do me ten times! Besides, how could I stab him when I can't even bear to kill a chicken?"

# PART II

*In which I, Mother's certified interpreter, take the license and space to expand some thoughts and images of a general nature to connect Mother's hospital reports with other accounts, all with the aim of describing and analyzing as precisely as possible the space, period, and people surrounding Mother, which I can say from my forensic viewpoint, after meticulous monitoring and systematic notation, influenced the development of her remarkable, somewhat mystical illness.*

*The reprimand for trying to organize a collection*
*(which is how good but overly arbitrary initiatives are ended)*

MOTHER WAS HURT by the reprimand she received. The hurt wrenched her from within, and it made her lose her composure and contentment. She did not realize that she needed to accept the reprimand inside because that way she could let go of it and be free again. She still protested inside and resisted, and as long as that went on she could not be free because she was constantly bound to the event. She thought it was the nurse who reprimanded her that bound her to the event, but that was incorrect. She bound herself to it, and as soon as she realized that she would be able to be completely free again.

She thought that by feeling hurt she was being true to herself, but actually she was not doing anything good for herself and not being true to herself. She was sticking to her self-image, which was an illusion and, as a picture, it was finite and limiting. Each time she realized that the image of herself she was true to did not exist at all or was unimportant, a huge space would open up inside her, much larger than she imagined. It was the space of the universe, love, and God's presence, which would descend into her with the lifting of that latch.

*Playing with words is dangerous*
*(it would be more sensible to say nothing at all)*

OF ALL THE patients at the hospital, Mother was the most self-possessed. That was because no one had bashed her and she was not full of sorrow and pent-up rage. Her illness came from the doctors once, long ago, removing her gateway of the universe. When a woman's gateway of the universe is excised she dies, even if she is still physically alive. Doctors do not reflect on that, instead they violently cut out women's gateways of the universe. That can leave them sad and depressed—they believe they are now worthless because their greatest treasure, that which made them women, and that from where all life came, has been forcibly cut away. Doctors think that if they excise something from a human being it will then be healthy, but that is wrong. Nothing has ever been cured with a scalpel—it only cuts short and downsizes that which protruded because it needed help, love, understanding, and forgiveness.

*The open secret of the doctor's envelope,*
*the gateway of the universe*

THE DOCTOR WHO excised Mother's gateway of the universe took the money in the envelope. Father gave a lot of money to that doctor, who was reputed to be the best carver of the human body. He was able to list all the body's organs. He had read so many works and textbooks and written such long research papers, which he presented at such venerable scientific gatherings, that the real human being had become as distant from him as the farthest point in space.

He knew bodies, dissected and bloody, and they were all the same, equally disgusting and repulsive. They had no names, just the amount of money in the envelope that designated the particular body, but the body itself was worthless. Everything that was of any worth could fit into a medium-size envelope, and the more there was in the envelope, the better, the values increased and ultimately drew level with the worthlessness of the dissected bodies.

When he had bought himself everything he desired so he could feel like a king who never laid hands on a wet rag to wipe mud off his shoes, the doctor began to sense the worthlessness of the envelopes, and not only them. Then Father and Mother came along, with a bulging envelope, and it began all over again. The bloody knives and scissors regained their true smell and color, and Mother too became a number—the amount in the envelope.

Things ended the way they did, and since they are over, there is no point speaking about them. Everything that is said or thought about the doctor and his envelopes is now superfluous because the envelopes are long since empty, and since they have long been emptied there is no point speaking about them anymore because they do not exist. Possibly they were only a figment of the imagination even when they existed, just as the doctor was a figment, and Mother's operation too. Everything, everything was a figment, and it is best that it stay that way, buried at the bottom of a putrid pit together with the doctor's coat, glasses, framed certificates of achievement, and Mother's gateway of the universe, through which I personally slipped out of Mother's womb one hot day.

TATJANA GROMAČA

*Happy birthday, Miss Fluffy!*

IT WAS MOTHER's birthday. She bought a big bar of chocolate at the hospital canteen. After lunch, which that day consisted of boiled kale with a large frankfurter and a piece of bread, Mother celebrated by sharing the chocolate with all the women in her room. She dressed up festively for the day in a new tunic with stripes of different colors. But the best thing of all was that the other women, following Mother's lead, sang songs after the chocolate and soft drinks.

"We sang 'A Little House on the Hill,' 'The Babbling Brook,' and 'Last Night after Dark.' Later we also sang a few hymns. A young nurse who's in the church choir joined in. The women could hardly wait to sing. Afterward we talked, as usual, about recipes, winter preserves and pickles, husbands, children . . . It was lovely!"

The next day, Mother became a worker. Occupational therapy. She signed on at the hospital's workshop for producing pillows. There she took mended pillowcases and stuffed them with imitation down, a fluffy synthetic material that resembled foam or snow. All sorts of things happened there, and some of the patients even fell in love because there were both men and women at the workshop.

"At half past ten we have a half-hour break, and we get coffee and soft drinks. Then we work until lunchtime. They feed us like in a hotel. Today there was tomato soup and fish. I gave my fish to the lady who smokes LM, but I still came out ahead. I got another bowl of tomato soup! After lunch we gathered in the lounge and a nurse read to us for an hour. Today's reading was about emotions."

When there are a lot of people in one place they can become bewildered. Often there is no good feeling if there are a lot of people in one place. Only music can create a good mood in that place and change people completely so that they suddenly stop hating one another, and themselves, and begin to live as divine souls. Then they sing and begin to radiate a divine love for everyone, not only those they know and feel close to. Song cleanses the soul like tears if it is pure and calls to love, not to bloody battle.

"Today I worked at the pillow workshop again. I tore and plucked at the fluffy down that goes in the pillows, and when it was time for our break two musicians came from the other workshop, with a guitar and an accordion. They played, and we sang and danced, a lot of songs. 'On the Boulevard,' 'Pretty Mara Went to Market,' 'Mirjana,'—that was for the head doctor, whose name is Mirjana—and 'Oh Ana, oh Anikins' for the head nurse, whose name is Anica. She came and listened to us. People sang and danced, although many of them are seriously ill and not feeling well. When people have the will to live, even when they're feeling wretched and sick, that will is there, and it's so strong. One day I watched a mother who came to visit her sick, mentally handicapped daughter, and changed her pajamas. She had bought her a new pair, terry cloth. That was terrible to see because her daughter is young but can't change her own clothes, and the mother changed her, one part of the body after another. That really saddened me. I cried for ten minutes."

*More bugs under the rug*

SINCE NO ONE believed anyone or anything because it was considered that neither truth nor the divine existed in people and that everyone was false and implicated in lies and evil in one way or another, people harbored a lot of bitterness and hatred toward everyone. No one believed anyone or anything and the accumulated suspicions and bad thoughts culminated in rage and anger, and also in the desire to see the Other crushed as one's worst enemy, and by no means to kiss and embrace them as brother or sister.

Everyone thought that they, and those closest to them in their living environment, were more or less secure, but sometimes not even that. If they felt secure in their environment, they nurtured the conviction that sincerity and honesty existed only within their circle, and that everything beyond it was insincere and dishonest. Therefore they listened to all others with a great dose of suspicion, gauging and weighing every word they spoke and every gesture they made. Image and tone were especially important, what kind of face someone had, and especially how they dressed, and whether their air reflected the place in society they had been allocated.

Tone was important because often it was not what was said that was relevant, but the way in which it was said and whether that demonstrated the power and rule of the strong, or submission and obedience. Everything was so simply ordered in facile opposites that there was no room for nuance and for people who reflected subtly and viewed reality and themselves in many different ways, and not only no room but also no need, and therefore anyone who viewed things in a slightly more complex way was free to pack their bags and hit the road—good riddance—or simply languish with the other bugs swept under the dusty rug.

A burlesque took place on the stages, in which actors, quite detached from the rest of the world, bestowed one another the greatest prizes and epithets. Genius and geniuses abounded, and everyone was a born and hereditary talent who could have the world at their feet if only they were interested.

And again, at the same time, everyone could hardly wait to detect an error in others, after careful study, because finding the errors in others was the only thing that could give them a scrap of joy. That was because everyone had been restrained from childhood from thinking, behaving, and speaking freely, and because, from an early age, the life in them had been crushed—the soul that wanted to live and develop inside them had been stifled.

Through systematic intimidation, bans, fear, and punishment when they were children, people's aspiration to become what they are was nipped in the bud, and they went on living semi-withered lives, consoling themselves that everyone else lived the same way and that it could not be otherwise.

The bugs under the rug that were sufficiently hardy to resist and were not afraid of punishment, blackmail, or intimidation were considered completely dead and withered. If the bugs, despite their predicament, managed to produce something of value under the rug, something that bore witness to the living fiber within their beings, the whole public above the rug would hastily shove it even farther under the rug so no one would notice, see, or hear.

Because the closer someone was to the truth, the more valuable their fabric was, whatever material they worked in, even scrap metal if that was close to real life and the people. Even if it seemed completely contrived, it had a force that could be recognized within those withered, sad little souls close to God and close to death, who, if they managed to retain a fragment of divine nobility of spirit in themselves, were able to sustain themselves in silence and secrecy with what they produced.

Everyone believed that people did things purely out of self-interest. They always looked for someone's personal advantage in everything, and if they could not find it, again they could not accept that there was none. It was in no way acceptable to any normal person for there to be someone who did things without self-interest, and if someone did do something without obvious personal advantage blinking on the surface they believed all the more fervently that there must be some special, great, secret scheme that everyone was willing to wait an especially long time for—years—because this was an exceptional, extraordinary advantage that would resound like a bomb one day.

I reflected on that, too, every time we cleared the creaky iron barrier, like at small railroad crossings and stations, and entered the hospital complex. It was orderly like a landscaped garden, and among the many firs, pines, oaks, weeping willows, birches, chestnuts, beeches, hazels, and poplars there were no wolves, foxes, or bears, nor graceful peacocks, antelopes, and gazelles, just the fat shadows of quite ordinary people who roamed the enclosed area like waddling ducks, sometimes draped in long robes, sometimes in dark, monochrome coats or, like Mother, in a winter jacket with the hood trimmed with imitation fur that bobbed and rocked in the wind like a vivacious squirrel's tail.

Gray winter vapors like steam from a heavy pot simmering came down on the heads of the laconic inhabitants of the hospital buildings, who, with gray faces and even grayer, deep looks, inhaled the gray fumes of narrow cigarettes. They were disillusioned soldiers who had fought for the honor of the homeland, which later cheated and betrayed them, who had literally walked over dead bodies and seen rotting corpses, which they themselves had often rent with their knives and gunstocks in the belief that it was for some purpose, for the sake of higher ideals, which they never doubted.

All the things their souls and bodies endured in the war came out in their dreams afterward. Their dreams were outright nightmares, which no one wanted to hear about because no one had time for that, and everything was hushed up and covered up by a handful of pills: white, red, and yellow-blue, thick or slim, elongated or rounded.

The hospital was full of such people, just as it was full of people without identity, who had to renounce their past, origin, and name, like Russian or Polish Jews seventy years earlier, in order to adapt to a new system of values, within which it was best for them not to exist, or rather for them to take a handful of white, red, and yellow-blue pills and sleep like the bears and small, furry beavers in some national park.

And so similar illnesses came together and condemned people to understanding friendship with those who had been on opposite sides during the insane war, because the soldiers had killed, raped, and eviscerated the bodies of those whose genetic makeup and blood count were incompatible with the grand designs for a brave new world in the greater region—pure and purged of all sundry, suspicious, smelly foreign bodies.

But everyone was a first among equals in the hospital and its immediate surroundings. No one felt a need to speak about those terrible days because everyone was subdued by pills, so they dragged their heavy shoes in silence with bowed heads like worn-out prisoners after a long day of physical labor. That is how it looked, but it was not always so grim and black because now and then, as Mother reported, there was singing and dancing, and with song and dance everything else is forgotten and the soul turns to divine, golden heights, where harmony, purity, and goodness prevail, and where no one cares about origin and where one might belong geographically because, viewed from those heights, there is no rhyme or reason to questions of that type.

*The genesis of fear, through the figure of the father-God*

MOTHER WOULD NOT have been so ill if there had not existed something even deeper than soldiers and wars. I always reflected on that when the heavy iron barrier at the hospital went down behind our old Škoda. I thought hard, trying to penetrate Mother's bones and get to the marrow. There, I believed, lay hidden the secret of her illness and the secret of everything that took place around Father and Mother's castle. It seemed to me that I always only found fear in Mother's bones, time and again. I studied all the minutiae and nuances of her bone mass attentively and in detail, checking my analyses and comparing them with hospital records kept by Mother's doctor. At the end of all roads and searches I had to submit some kind of specialist report to myself in order to prove that, despite the apparent intricacy, it was possible to arrive at fairly clear answers.

*Specialist report*
*(a technique combining in-depth bone analysis*
*and the hospital record cards)*

MOTHER'S FATHER DROVE fear into her bones. That was while she was still a very small girl. That fear entered her bones and fiber so deeply that it never left her again, all her life. That fear became part of her, it became her very self. She dreaded her father's punishment, every day and all her life. Her father was God Himself, and all good things that came to Mother were thanks to him, while all bad things came by her doing. There were actually no bad things—they never existed because Mother satisfied the expectations of her father-God to the extent that everything she did was good and completely in line with what was demanded of her.

Possibly some things happened to Mother during her life that were not entirely to her liking, but, according to her father's stance in the whole business of raising his eldest daughter, bad things did not exist. As such, what was not to her liking or what was perhaps a little bit bad, was swept under the rug.

Anything that did not meet the mark was stuffed away like that, and on the surface everything was bright and shiny, better than best, crystal clear and clean, like the house that Mother cleaned tirelessly every day, over and over again.

Mother kept her fear very well hidden. Everything was fine and excellent, and therefore it was not permissible for there to be any fear, because fear was bad. It was good that there always be a little fear, but not too much, and since Mother had too much of it, she herself did not need to know of its existence. For that reason, Mother was always loud and cheerful, and if by any chance she was not, she was nervous and furious. She always exuded intense emotions, precisely so as not to allow the quiet, delicate emotions under her skin, of which fear was one, to slither out from under the bed during the night like a thick black snake.

EVERYTHING MOTHER DID in life she did to satisfy her father because he was God, who created her and breathed life into her, like Moloch. Deferential gratitude was her duty. She owed him everything. He had fed and clothed her, and whenever she was ill he took her to the doctor, who vaccinated her. Her father put her through school, and he also fed her at the family table when she was already able to marry and go to another table. But her father was so generous as to keep her at his table until she produced a certificate written with a calligraphic flourish on cardboard to confirm that she was now an educated person.

Mother's father was by no means an extraordinary father, not even by being her God, considering he was just one of a million fathers who had been brought up in an identical way and raised their own progeny in an identical way. They passed on what they inherited without any real question, blindly accepting and following it. According to this idea, every man was God, even while he was in his mother's womb, and every woman was a disgrace, at least potentially, even while she was in her mother's womb.

Since every woman was a potential disgrace, she had to be treated with great caution as well as great stringency in order to drive great fear into her bones once and for all so she would never even think of doing anything shameful. These chaotic contradictions defined being a woman, and knotted Mother into the self she became, the self she embraced and loathed, celebrated and mourned.

Mother did not do anything shameful, of course. On the contrary, she was a paragon of virtue, and as such she earned God's—that is, her father's—blessing and affection. When he died, Mother sat on his deathbed, controlled by his still present beliefs. After his death, Mother continued to do everything she could to satisfy his expectations. Even when she had the face of a toothless old lady and a geriatric limp, she was still a small girl who sought signs of approval in the eyes of her strict father.

Mother lived her whole life without ever growing up because she always strove for recognition and honor. Like the majority of other people, who also considered they were grown up, although growing up and maturation never really took place within them, she believed recognition and honor were tops and the top of the tops.

But Mother's aspiration for recognition and honor was only an aspiration for recognition and honor by her father-God, and although he strove for recognition and honor himself and was the bearer of several honorary epaulettes, he was never profligate in giving recognition and honor.

Since Mother was so exemplary and respectable and perhaps no longer needed to make a special effort in this regard, she concentrated part of her efforts on those who were not exemplary and respectable and whose behavior clashed in every way with the standards set by the rule of her father-God. Mother reacted quite instinctively to everything that was outside or even contrary to those standards, and sometimes she even pointed a finger at those whose behavior she deemed improper, like a child might when playing at being an adult.

"The two men sat and played their accordions, and two women from our ward sat next to them, one beside each, leaning her head on the man's shoulder. One of the men played 'A Gorgeous Raven Haired Girl' for the woman who had black hair, and for the other, who was blonde, he played 'A Blonde Once Beguiled Me.' The women didn't do anything, but each rested her head on the shoulder of one of the men, and they grinned and smirked as if they were tipsy. Everyone knows what it means to lean your head on a man's shoulder—it's a clear message! Still, I decided not to tell the nurse later what the women did after the music—what happened at the ward when the accordion players were there."

But Mother was not such a moralist. Sometimes she had understanding for love and sex, but only if they took place within the institution of marriage. When, as a very young woman, she borrowed *Lady Chatterley's Lover* from the town library, it was obvious that her father, who saw everything, just like God sees everything, given that he regularly went to the library to inquire about the books his daughter borrowed, would take the harshest measures to ensure that such books never be read again. They had never brought any good to anyone!

"Several days ago there was a talk about love, and one about sex. I raised my hand in the discussion after each talk because I have experience of love, and I have experience of sex too. In any case, I never knew that sex was so important for the family. They told us in the talk that sex in marriage is very important. I had no idea.

"Actually, when I had that big test several years ago, before I retired, I had to answer around seven hundred questions, and fifty of the seven hundred were about sex. God, how important sex is!

"When your father wanted us to have another child, I didn't, but his wish prevailed. He wanted us to have two children because he grew up without a brother or sister. You were already big and going to school when we had your sister, and your father was afraid you could be involved in a traffic accident. You walked to school every day along that busy road, and Father was afraid something could happen to you. So he thought it would be good for us to have a second child because it would be a kind of guarantee that one of the two children would survive and outlive us, although we didn't want anything to happen to you, obviously."

Father certainly hoped the second child would be a boy, since the first was not and he was surrounded by women and did not have an heir—one who would carry on his family name and line until the end of the world. No daughter could make up for or replace a son, not even if she could drive a car, go to the horse races, fish, or drive a tractor. Not even a daughter who played soccer very well and cheered for the same team as the father could be any help.

A daughter was simply worthless because one day she would leave, take her husband's name, and become part of his line, departing her own and forgetting it, unless her eyes retained a quiver of fear and a desire for the admiration that she could perhaps one day still win from her father.

*Specialist report on Father, or rather on Mother,*
*or a bit of both*

JUST AS MOTHER believed that her father-God punished her every time she as much as thought of doing something bad, so Father believed that God was punishing him—because of all the bad things that happened to him. Father and Mother believed God meted out punishment, and they lived all their lives in that conviction. There was a force here stronger than the law of communicating vessels, than the canals of deep subterranean watercourses and wells connected at some unknown point. Still, now and then they would relax a little and sometimes go beyond the box.

In those moments, Mother and Father's shared soul could be glimpsed, as broad as the widest Russian steppes, a soul that loved and understood the world, was deep and humanistic, and could be free and untrammeled. A soul that laughed and sang, that loved and knew it could be happy and fulfilled, and deserved to be. It was a poetic soul, one that wanted Father to become a musician and Mother a folk singer and dancer.

In fear of God, and wishing to appease their domestic gods (Mother her father-God and Father his mother, the Virgin Mary) neither Father nor Mother permitted their soul to flee the box into which their domestic gods had stuffed them—to leave it for good. Maybe that was not even practicable, but now and then their soul came out on its own and appeared in all of its splendor and exuberance, only to be hastily squeezed back into the box afterward, in fear that some little piece could be left jutting out and perhaps betray them to all the others from whom they hid, and they hid from everyone because God was omnipresent and saw absolutely everything.

Sometimes, even involuntarily, their soul fought against the box into which others had crammed it. Then Father and Mother created scenes, and punishment swiftly ensued as a result. Limitations were to be obeyed and people had to knuckle under to each one—Father and Mother learned that message the hard way. Whoever had the power to impose limitations was right, even if the limitations they imposed were completely crazy, sick, and insane, entirely to the detriment of people's health and sanity, perhaps sometimes of Father and Mother themselves, and then they had to confess with a straight face and calm heart that precisely such villains and criminals were right.

And not only did they have to confess, with faces bloodied by their blows or dripping with their spit, that the villains and criminals were absolutely right, but Father and Mother were also expected with every gesture and action to enthusiastically endorse their rectitude and everything they stood for, and to perish for every lofty idea they stood for with their noble blows and magnanimous spits in the face.

*A town on antidepressants*

IN THE TOWN Father and Mother came from people were on antidepressants. Everyone took different drugs to be able to accept all they had to accept, in order to pass over all they had to pass over, to forget all they tried to forget and, at the end of the day, to become indifferent, passive observers of the history of general illness and the general madness in a small, pastoral environment.

There were all sorts of men, beginning with those who rode old bicycles and pegged the wide legs of their gray trousers with clothespins so they would not get caught in the spokes. There were mostly men like that, and they rode their rusty bicycles in winter too, while hoarfrost gathered on their clothes and the red-string bags of potatoes slung over the racks at the back.

Sometimes a plastic fertilizer sack lay over the rack, filled with empty plastic bottles, because a lot of the men with clothespins on their trouser legs eked out a living by rooting around in trash with their bare hands, looking for empty plastic bottles that they could sell for less than a kuna each. There was a right plague of such "prospectors," who emerged at first light, before sunrise, from small brick houses or cardboard hovels wrapped in plastic, wire paper, cardboard, and Styrofoam, as well as empty egg cartons, which have always been good insulation against the noise and commotion of a busy town.

Sometimes there was a small basket at the back, like in big cities all around the world, with a dirty turnip rolling around next to three withered cabbage leaves picked up off the concrete floor under the stalls of the town market.

Everything was connected to the men on rusty bicycles. The town was also filled with drugged people who slept night and day in their houses and high-rises so as not to have to watch all they were bound to see, and there were also those who dozed at the counters in stores and desks in various specialized agencies, where top-level decisions were made, including about who would be punished for war crimes or would miraculously continue to be spared such punishment.

Everyone in the town had to take antidepressants, a huge amount and continuously, because something had happened there in the recent past that no one was ever allowed to admit because the very admission that something so appallingly terrible and inhuman had happened in the recent past would be perceived as a betrayal of sorts.

Therefore everyone lived every day as if that had not happened, but they could only live like that if they took antidepressants day after day because what happened was so ubiquitous in that town that, despite all efforts, it emanated from all the walls and houses, from all the parks and rivers, from all the warehouses and the concrete factory, just as it emanated from the bodies and clothes of the people who lived in the drugged town, regardless of how freshly and expensively they dressed and what unusual, liberal-minded hairstyles they wore.

Apart from the people on antidepressants, the town was also home to a great many stray dogs. Every day, those strays roamed the streets, alleys, and underpasses, retired along the riverbanks, and floated in abandoned fishing boats like frigid sphinxes with piercing, hypnotic eyes. Those mongrels were so uncannily threatening that no one dared to do anything to them—to call the sanitation department or the dogcatchers, or to raise the question of their culling or deportation to irradiated areas or minefields, where they would all die within just a few days.

"If anyone had ventured to count those stray dogs, they would have ascertained with horror that there were thousands of the grim-looking creatures, with fur filthy from slinking through all imaginable and unimaginable, noisome and inaccessible places, where human feet surely, out of caution, had not stepped for years." Those were the words noted in a local almanac that recorded all manner of phenomena important to the life of the town on antidepressants.

Why there were suddenly so many stray dogs on the streets of the town on antidepressants, no one knew exactly. There were rumors, to be sure, that it was somehow connected to the consequences of the wartime killings, with the mysterious disappearance of several hundred fellow townsfolk, ordinary citizens who were swallowed up by the whistling of nightly warning sirens, and with the feral pigs, which had been roaming the nearby fields and burned villages for years, transmitting infectious diseases to those who approached them out of ignorance or frivolity.

There was gossip about the feral pigs in the nearby villages and fields. Some said it was good they had spread because their voracious jaws broke down and devoured the already decomposed bodies, thus eliminating the traces of possible war crimes. The pigs devoured not only the putrid matter but also the bones, remains of fabric, and clothes of the corpses, such that the forensic teams came away empty-handed. All they could now do was establish that there had not been any crimes in those villages and fields and that the alleged crimes were just a crude fabrication of hostile propaganda.

No one could say with certainty what connection that had to the stray dogs that roamed the streets every day, but at the mention of those dogs everyone nodded toward the villages, fields, and forests, or rather toward the feral pigs, without trying to give a logical explanation.

The stray dogs often had their sights on the big metal trash barrels, the contents of which they could only get at by first turning them upside down. That usually happened at night, when the strays were out foraging and the air was filled with the crashing and banging of overturned barrels, as if the wartime shelling and bombing continued in those acoustic forms, after which the dogs' fetid, foul jaws tore apart pieces of trash on the asphalt in search of a plastic sausage wrapper, an empty can of beans, or rotten chicken livers and brains.

Another of their daily targets was the meat processing factory and its unfenced waste heap. Every day they swarmed to pick at the mangled bones of calves, cows, and pigs, and they fought there among themselves, drawing blood if necessary, so that the factory, on top of everything else, also had to deal with the occasional fresh corpses of stray dogs killed in those tooth-and-claw fights.

Near the mined villages and areas inhabited by a semi-literate population, who in the meantime, since the war, had learned to drop voting slips into ballot boxes but still lived on muddy farms and went to milk cows in smelly sheds full of manure, there arose a Center for Peace and the Fight Against War, where some of the most savagely efficient wartime executioners and killers cultivated a newfound peace-loving streak.

Since the war had ended a long time ago and there was no longer any point or prestige in ordering the killing of a whole range of civilians who they did not like or feel comfortable with, and since one of the new imperatives was to facilitate people quickly forgetting what they were still proud of deep down but was a kind of stigma for some of those in high positions, the warmongers, profiteers, and others to blame for the war turned overnight into minions of the peace movement.

That was a new image for new times, and it called for new marketing and new slogans such as "Tolerance will overcome hatred and violence" or "Accepting diversity enables growth and social progress." It was sufficient to jump on the bandwagon of the so-called "peace alliance" that spread throughout the world, and every emperor could order new clothes, or rather every wolf could don a sheepskin, and those who knew the emperor or the wolf from before pretended not to notice.

Despite all this, the large clock in the town's central park ran perfectly and faultlessly, and the slow movement of its hands, gilded with 14-karat gold, could be heard all the way to the nearby suburb, as well as the murmur of the town's fountain, at the top of which thrashed a huge golden fish the size of a pike.

That was because fishing had become one of the town's main postwar pursuits. Fishing was just the right activity for frayed nerves, which were soothed by pharmaceuticals, and, again, the idle hands needed something to do.

So from morning till the dark of night, the levees along the rivers and the small sandy banks were dotted with flocks of anglers, like strange dark green birds, who stood like the statues of a fountain holding their fishing rods. They wore army camouflage uniforms and waders so they could go out into the water, whose level was already low.

The river was periodically poisoned by chemicals and effluent, not to mention the air inhaled by the already drugged population that came from contaminated factories, which had been ransacked and abandoned and now just served as a backdrop for the incineration of toxic substances brought in semis and freezer trucks from Europe's civilized countries. And yet fishing, anglers, and the fish caught in the river became the town's symbol, and its pride.

That is why there is a golden fish writhing at the top of the jet of the town's tallest fountain, in the central park, right next to the cathedral as upright as the town's pride and hard-won freedom.

TATJANA GROMAČA

*From a papyrus scroll sealed in a beer bottle fished out of one of the malodorous rivers in the town on antidepressants*

SINCE PEOPLE HAD trodden down everything great and grand in themselves, they also began to despise themselves. That was the beginning of great contempt for everyone, but most of all for those who, against all odds, still lived their lives based on love, truth, and noble-mindedness.

The most important thing was to lie, lie, and lie, and to have cards hidden up one's sleeve for every occasion. And never to wear one's heart on that sleeve, not even for one's husband or wife. To live in trepidation of being hurt and always at risk of being betrayed. To be restrained and constantly take precautions, to be a balding old cat that washes its fur with its dirty, greasy tongue, while eyeing its terrified quarry that timidly peeks around the corner.

Man had become wolf to man, and maybe he always was. Only for Easter and Christmas did everyone put on a show of solidarity, but even then they directed their glances more at the plates than at their fellows.

People always emphasized that the most important thing was to be healthy, and more than anything else they said they wished one another the best of health. At the same time, they lived as if they did not care at all about their own health and actually wanted to undermine and ruin it as soon as possible, as if they had never been healthy. They crammed unhealthy food and poisons into themselves, and when something began to hurt they went to doctors, who in an illegible and inscrutable hand, for free or a small surcharge, liberally prescribed them colorful pills or syrups. These mysterious drugs instantly relieved their pain and suppressed the symptoms, usually until the next event, when it started all over again. The only difference was that the number and variety of medications increased over time.

People perceived their body as something unknown, foreign, and alien, a machine that at a certain stage of life inevitably needed servicing, and later the replacing of particular parts. That was perceived as quite natural—the cutting of parts of the body was more natural than the body itself, which was perceived as unnatural or removed from nature.

At the mention of cutting a part of the body, which was called an "operation," people all closed ranks and unanimously uttered dark, sympathetic tones, like when women at the hairdresser's lean their heads together under their dryer hoods to whisper to one another the bittersweet news of someone's marital infidelity, serious illness, or death.

# PART III

*In which semi-scientific and semi-medical analyses of the general illness of the place and time gather momentum. This chapter also goes into greater depth in analyzing Mother's character, now viewed from a broader perspective, in which she is a sample specimen, planted like a seed in a jar so that through careful monitoring one might be able to ascertain changes, development, and sprouting, in other words the platitudes of one such plant— Mother—or any person. All, of course, for furthering the realization that people are much more similar and alike than we usually think and muse, which is to say that Mother as an individual gradually declines in importance to make way for reflections on people in general.*

*The hospital, a divine light, and finally,*
*almost always, the ego*

AT LEAST THE hospital was always within reach. But it became ever busier there and admission ever harder—and it was almost like winning the lottery to get a place there, in other words a bed, where the person with the wounded soul could rest their head.

There were so many people wounded in the soul and who wanted to walk with other wounded souls around the hospital grounds, gather fallen acorns or crushed cigarette butts, and quickly stick them into the pockets of their hospital gowns that they now needed even better and steadier nerves to help them endure the time until their turn came and they could go to the hospital.

Not everything was milk and honey in the hospital, but at least there were others who were similar and who bore a secret in their hearts that they did not wish to speak about because they felt that by doing so they would hurt too many people, or they thought that speaking about the secrets would lead to changes in their own lives—changes they were not prepared for.

Therefore they kept those big and terrible secrets concealed in their hearts, like money in hidden safes, and the more time passed, the more the secrets galled them because over time they grew and grew, swelling with the desire to be released. That was not allowed to happen, and the secrets and the soul inside them hurt them more and more, to the extent that they felt they would burst asunder in pain and mute silence and end up at the bottom of an abyss, where was nothing but eternal night and eternal sleep.

There are remedies for eternal sleep, too. Perhaps the problem is only a lack of iron in the blood, and therefore the person lacks strength and forever wants to sleep. If the problem is a lack of iron in their blood, it is sufficient to stick a nail into an apple, leave it there overnight, and eat the apple the next day. That way you can put more iron into your blood and get back the strength you thought was lost.

It is the same with the mind, which can also become completely lost, and that happens precisely to the most intelligent people, precisely because they are mentally so alive, which weighs on their mind and galls them from time to time, such that ultimately they can no longer think, and often they can only talk and talk, or perhaps only look on in silence, cry, and throw their arms around the neck of a harnessed horse and empathize with it, like Friedrich Nietzsche did with the horse on the street in Turin.

It was like that with a philosophy teacher and a teacher of literature and history. The great pressure in their minds made them constantly talk and talk. She and he walked about the hospital complex or sat cross-legged by the green fireplace in the wall of the hospital corridor.

The other patients thought the two teachers talked nonsense, but that was because they spoke the truth. The truth often seemed like bullshit because almost no one spoke it out loud, so no one paid attention to it, except perhaps the two or three stokers from the auxiliary building with their dark blue coats and checkered scarves around their necks, or the two fat cleaning ladies, whose laddered nylons and pastel pink aprons showed when they stooped down to sweep little piles of trash into their plastic dustpans.

The philosophy teacher and the teacher of literature and history mostly talked the same nonsense, the claptrap that was going around about the hit lists for liquidating civilians during the most recent war, which had taken place twenty years ago, and which everyone pretended they had never heard of, and that they had forgotten everything that happened then. The two teachers wanted to convince whoever passed within earshot through the hospital grounds or went past the green fireplace in the corridor that it was impossible for everyone to have forgotten all those things because they themselves remembered people who disappeared overnight, like in Stalin's purges. Some had been their neighbors. With others, they had sat together in the high school teacher's lounge, and some of those who disappeared had been their students.

They wanted to convince everyone around them of the truthfulness of those stories, but no one would listen to them because everyone basically believed the two teachers had lost their minds. Their stories only seemed amusing now and then to the two stokers, the janitor, and the fat cleaning ladies, who cast amorous glances at the stokers leaning against the frame of the basement door as they bent over plastic buckets full of foamy water to rinse their washcloths filthy with cigarette butts and mud.

The teacher of philosophy constantly spoke about history having repeated itself in the town and the whole region because major crimes had occurred again, like those that took place in the great war seventy years earlier, which everyone also pretended had not taken place and pretended they knew nothing about, and it had stayed that way up until this day. She said that the crimes happened again precisely because the previous ones had not been spoken about, just as these new ones were not spoken about. Therefore she now talked about the recent crimes, mainly so that it might prevent them from happening again.

"Because if these crimes aren't spoken about loudly and clearly now, like I'm speaking to you here, you can be certain that they'll happen again, and much sooner than you think," the philosophy teacher said.

When she had spoken, everyone sniggered and winked to each other as if they had heard a good, slightly smutty joke.

AS FAR AS Mother was concerned, she was one of the most privileged patients in the hospital because she was allowed to stay longer than most. That was because, unlike other patients who suffered from the same illness, Mother was quite unable to establish a balance between her own lows and highs. In one moment Mother was on a high, and in that state she could be especially interesting. She talked constantly, even about things she had carefully kept secret all her life, for example that Father had once carried her in his arms through a canal and across fields of young barley, cabbages, and pumpkins. Mother did not go into details in that account, maybe because she sensed Father's shame and discomfort. In other words, when Mother was on a high she did not feel shame, like people who are drunk feel no shame at things they otherwise would, so they are not ashamed to sing loudly or talk about love and affection.

Apart from having the freedom to speak about things she otherwise did not dare to, Mother was so free as to think better of herself than she usually did. But that was a dubitable space for everyone else: Did Mother think of herself so highly the rest of the time too, or was it her highs that whisked her away to lofty elevations, where she saw herself as a living monument miraculously still in motion?

As well as Mother's voice apparatus being turned on and amplified to unimaginable proportions almost all the time, except when she was sleeping, her highs intensified her sense of life's positive values. So Mother was not capable of seeing anything bad, and when she did, she behaved like a veritable savant—she understood and loved what was bad, and she advised those who suffered from that evil to be patient, with love and understanding.

On a high and on drugs, Mother gained what can be called a "divine perspective." She was able to view everything from a distant and most exalted plane, without ignoble motives, schadenfreude, and sarcasm, without gossip and reproach. Mother no longer had any need of ignoble human feelings, negativity, and fears. She needed none of that because when she was on a real high she dispelled all evil. She was calm and tranquil, full of love and joy, and there were no earthly events at that time in which Mother was not capable of seeing good.

It is fair to say that everyone envied Mother in a way. She had days such as ordinary people only experience once or twice in their lifetime—usually just before death, they say—when all petulance and preoccupations vanish into insignificance and the soul rises up from the mists to a lofty clearing, where it sees only the wellspring of life and its full meaning, and where it is illuminated by divine love and the grace of its gentle resplendence.

But there was also a dark side to Mother's highs. Something surfaced that wise philosophers spoke of, for example Pascal: "All men wish to rule." That is how Mother's ego, especially in that elevated state, and its wish to rule over others really

TATJANA GROMAČA

manifested. Being so high, her ego spread its wings above all around her to such an extent that nothing else could be seen beneath those aquiline pinions. Nothing could be seen or heard except Mother's singular voice.

*Mother as an exemplar of several human truisms*

FORTUNATELY THERE WERE still some people whom Mother shrank from and humbly folded those wings. They were people of authority, mostly in uniform. The doctor in her white coat and white clogs, the blue-trousered nurse, the policeman, the firefighter. Would Mother perhaps even have obeyed a chimney sweep?

Mother's deep-seated fear of her supreme leader and authority, her father-God, made her terribly afraid of everything that wore the robe of power. In view of that fear, Mother never grew up, because if she had, she would have realized that authority is playacting and fiction, that the embodiment of power is a façade for impotence and fear, and that there is no greatness behind the sense of possession because greatness resides only in the dissolution of and departure from all relations of ownership, from every will to appropriate things, even if only a moldy cabbage.

Ridding oneself of the will to possess could be a step toward freedom and the possibility of personal growth, but Mother had not yet reached that stage. She was at the source of innocence and purity, in her early childhood, where there could admittedly be trivial squabbles and childish spite, the desire to rule, a little envy, and insecurity overlaid with a lot of prattle, but all that was innocent and pure compared with the world of adults, in which Mother lived a large part of her life but which she did not get to know. She truly believed she was very much grown-up and that she understood life, and so, like the majority of other immature adults who subordinated their life to satisfying the expectations of others, most often authoritarian members of the family, Mother was inclined to lecture.

Since she believed—or wished to assure others and herself—that she was indeed mature and that life in its full ripening had passed through her, leaving traces that she as a grown-up person was prepared to interpret, Mother was eternally preaching and pontificating, even to her superiors. Everyone got their lesson and was told what they had coming to them.

Mother was constantly giving people gratuitous advice on how to lead their lives, but the person whose ear those lessons were intended for never came up to thank her for her effort and give her a medal for reaching maturity and independence, emphasizing that she was now free to do whatever she wished and that she was fully responsible for her actions and decisions in life, independent of everyone.

Since her supreme authority never did that in his lifetime, Mother did what she had the habit and need of doing all her life, only now much more intensively because she was on a high. She continued along the same iron rail like a locomotive because she had no other track.

As such, Mother was unable to establish a balance, even with the help of drugs, because she was never balanced, considering that she had never been "her own." She was the daughter of her father, whom she served devotedly all her life, trying hard to carn his recognition, or at least his praise. How could she be "her own" in illness when she had never been it in health?

The best thing that could happen to Mother in her illness was that she be in rapture, not of her own, no longer her father's, but of God, as she fancied Him, and of the angels. Therefore Mother loved her imaginary God, and that is why she went to church. There she found a small part of the atmosphere she now possessed in her soul and thoughts, cleansed of all evil.

In addition to all that, hymns were sung at church. The singing took her to the very gates of paradise, after which she would slowly, or suddenly, plunk back down onto the hard floor of reality.

*An enchanted castle, a villa, and the patience
of the rescued flakes*

IN REALITY, THE hospital was waiting for Mother, and she continued to spend spells of time there. It was a marvelous hospital that did not look like a medical institution at all, but more resembled a magical castle from a fairy tale. Everything in that castle-hospital was magical—even the chimney, the roof, the windows, the veranda, and the little flight of stairs leading up to the front door. The corridors and tiled fireplaces were magical, the lockers for keeping the patients' clothes were equally magical, as were the little locker keys that the enchanted people who came to stay in that castle-hospital wore on a piece of string around their wrists.

Around the enchanted castle there were other castles too, on knolls scattered through the forest. The forest was partly evergreen, partly deciduous, so there were leaves or thin green needles on some of the trees all year. A lot of snow fell in the forest in winter, and Mother walked over it with a green cap, red gloves, and a brown coat with the hood trimmed with imitation squirrel's fur, which hung down over her back.

Mother walked mainly when she went to church for Sunday mass or when she went to stuff the fluffy down into the small pillowcases. She called that down "flakes." She would say, "We stuffed flakes again today, I was stuffing those flakes."

When there was snow and when there was none at all, Mother's life was full of flakes. They were her natural element because she was also water, like flakes—she was the kind of water that constantly flows and whose inner roar from distant depths can be heard when it issues, heralding changes that will soon turn everything upside down—absolutely everything.

But more time still had to pass before then. How much time had to pass and how much time ever has to pass for something to happen that someone wants to happen—that is not for them to know. What a person needs to know, and what they need to be sure of, which will lend them tranquility, is that time will come with certainty, unavoidably, unless a person wishes to invoke it themselves through their own actions before the right time comes. If a person tries to speed up time, they will harm themselves and others around them because such brute acceleration will hamper harmony.

*A scene from the time before the serum of hatred was administered*

A VILLAGE WEDDING was taking place one rainy day. I had a small umbrella with pictures of tropical animals: a lion, a giraffe, a zebra, an elephant, a tiger, and a small monkey hanging from a branch—all of them creatures from Africa. It was pastoral and sad, backward and muddy, but there was nothing threatening about it. No one had guns in their mind at all, perhaps at most for a shot in the air to celebrate when the bride stepped out of the small, gray, boxy house into the muddy courtyard in her white party shoes. But even then, even then there was no reason for real pistols; only shotguns came into consideration, shotguns for the plump little sparrows and scatterbrained starlings from the orchard that simply could never peck their fill of the maize in the attic.

But that was long ago, before anyone's tea had been laced with the toxic serum of hatred. The hatred spread much later, when a very well-preserved illusion shattered. And then all hell broke loose, with all of its rings of evil. Some became killers; others were killed. Some survived to carry a fear inside them as great as the eye of a dead, rigid elephant.

*A person's fate—why it is not possible to live
without ideologies*

IN OTHERS' EYES, Mother and Father became two opposing armies. Those eyes saw them from the perspective of ideology because the majority adopted that view for fear of being accused of weakness, of lacking scorn and hatred. Now that one illusion had shattered, everyone rushed to embrace the illusion of pure origin, of blood and soil. It was a terrible thought for everyone to imagine that they could live without illusions, eye to eye with their own ego, because no one knew their own ego or had the courage to try and grasp it without illusions, fairy tales, and myths.

Those myths abounded with heroes of a majestic past, impeccable ancestors with pure roots, ancient progenitors and forebears, giants with broad shoulders and big, bony fingers, whose breath could bring down mountains, and whose guttural voices now resounded within the newly created state borders, echoing off cliffs, mountains, plains, and the sea like the *zaum* sound symbolism of a Tibetan chant for dispelling evil spirits.

According to those myths, there was no place for Mother within the newly created borders and ideologies because her roots were too branchy and cabbagey. A lot of mud clung to them, and probably putrid matter and worms as well. No one wanted to have such roots, not even Mother herself, but she was powerless. Nothing could be done about her roots if they were not as they should be; it was best to bury oneself deep in the ground and rot together with them.

*Hibernation as a protest against ideologies*

AND SO MOTHER dug herself in deep and hibernated, like an enchanted sleeping princess, for ten whole years.

And when she woke up one day after sleeping for ten years, there was no way she could catch up on everything she had slept through in that time. She wanted to see everyone she had not seen during all those years. She wanted to tell them all the things she had dreamed in that time and what she remembered in her dreams. She needed someone to pin a medal on her chest for merit because she thought she deserved it after sleeping an enchanted sleep for so long.

She honored herself with salvos of praise for holding out for so long and not taking her own life, thus saving the family from being marked by eternal shame. Those were her words. She spoke all the time because she wanted to fill the hiatus that had opened up inside her and around her during that long time— fill it with words. She thought that if she talked constantly she would prevent the hiatus of sorrow, lethargy, numbness, and sleep, which had enslaved her, from creeping up on her again. Constant speech was a sword she used to cut through the thick, thorny branches of fear, whose growth around her she dreaded.

Since she had been sad for so long, Mother now constant-ly wanted to be cheerful. She wanted every day to be like her birthday, when she would get presents and everyone she knew would phone to wish her many happy returns, and they would raise a glass in her name and she would be given big bunches of flowers so massive that they would completely conceal her face, on which everything was still in place apart from her teeth.

Instead of a frugal stew, she wanted to eat meat for lunch every day, and have cake for dessert, and in the evenings she wanted to down a thick smoothie made of two big ripe banan-as instead of a cup of tea without lemon. She wanted to knead dough and make cakes to show anyone who doubted it that she was healthy and capable. She would move heaven and earth to be mother, homemaker, and wife again.

The truth was that she could no longer be anywhere near as perfect as she was before. Now it was as if her eyes became cov-ered by a thin, gray-brown film that made things around her seem a little blurred and murky. At the same time, things were some-times small and crumpled, ragged, and insufficiently clean. But Mother did not notice this because of the film that covered her eyes, and for her everything she did and all the things around her seemed perfect, without a single flaw or weakness. That is how she saw all the close things that surrounded her, but also people—both herself and those farther afield.

That was a new, positive light she cast around herself, and it was unique in having no nuances.

At the same time, Mother fed off the pity she aroused in others. She constantly did all she could to stir the same inner chords in those around her, whose vibrations said they felt pity and com-passion toward her, that they ought to pity her for her hard fate. That was not difficult because it involved the same chords with everyone, which could be stirred by the same words. Mother

TATJANA GROMAČA

spoke completely identical words in conversation with entirely different people, and the entirely different people took the identical words in exactly the same way. That could be seen as proof that a person is a simple machine and that the most different people have levers inside them that are set in motion in entirely identical circumstances, and those movements produce the same reactions.

Mother put her words together in such a way that they could be taken identically by a muddy shepherd from the meadows, who never learned to read and write, and by the lawyer in the courtroom with a gold-banded watch on his wrist. Mother had a talent for forming her sentences like primitive peoples shaped clay figurines—big-bellied women with sagging breasts and scowling buffalos with sharp horns. Her words were therefore comprehensible to all, and everyone could see themselves reflected in them because they were like a colorfully framed mirror that returned an embellished image of the person who sought their reflection in it.

In that sense they actually more resembled the sun, which everyone took for granted and whose warmth sustained everyone, regardless of their status or standing.

But in general, people could not observe others without scrutinizing how much money they had, what kind of car they drove, and what schools they had attended. Most people could not view another person without taking a multitude of similar factors into account, by which people examined each other, by which they met each other, judged each other, and the men abducted each other's women. It all revolved around simple images and questions that sought constant affirmation from everyone that they were "normal" and well adapted to the general mold, which did not physically exist anywhere in reality but was omnipresent and managed to suck almost all living beings into itself.

The compassion she received from others created the feeling in Mother that she was loved and that, on account of her hard fate, she was exceptional and great at the same time. It gave her a feeling of power, with whose help she energetically hobbled among people, some of whom perhaps considered she should be ashamed of her illness and the nuances she no longer saw, and which constituted the rules of good behavior.

Now after those long ten years, in her own eyes, Mother was one of the most deserving and exemplary of people, which was not particularly unusual because we can assume that almost everyone thought of themselves like that, or at least every second person, except that unlike Mother, whose rules of good behavior had now got somewhat mixed up, they kept that carefully hidden.

Mother became inclined to emphasize that very often, but that did not automatically mean she was actually convinced of it. Rather, it is more likely she wanted to believe it, and we cannot really know if she actually thought that about herself, and we should rather doubt if she truly thought that. In any case, we can say that, like thousands and thousands of others, she wanted to receive acknowledgment, and by speaking about her merits she received it, in a way, from those who listened to her.

There were other rules of etiquette that Mother confused as well. Since she had come face to face with her own death and convinced herself of the existence of God, she became religious. When she went to church, Mother realized that all men are brothers, and in line with that she had a habit of approaching strangers, because, quite rightly, she did not perceive them as strangers, but as kindred spirits and in a way the same as her. In that sense, Mother set a precedent and it would be fair to say that she was a troublemaker, but, as things stood, a positive

TATJANA GROMAČA

troublemaker, because most people liked Mother coming up to them as brothers and sisters and addressing them with kind words and good wishes.

*I return to Mother: good men and bad,*
*according to the Croatian Renaissance writer*
*Marin Držić and according to Mother*

IN MOTHER'S EXPERIENCE, there existed only two sorts of people: those who live by the truth and those who live by the lie. Jesus Christ lived by the truth, as did the likes of John the Baptist and the Blessed Virgin Mary. Perhaps a few more lived by the truth, but it was especially hard to remember them. And yet Mother believed there were a lot of people who lived by the truth, but whose names and faces were unknown to her. She wanted to believe she also strove to live by the truth, which meant that very often, sometimes without knowing it, she drifted into lying, but then she did everything in her power to delve ever deeper in her conscience, trying to find the truth again and return to its resplendent clearing.

Living by the truth meant bliss and peace, a gentle shimmering on sunlit water. Living by the truth meant purity and a love that was unconditionally and infinitely extended to all, even those who considered they did not deserve it.

Living by the truth meant perfect inner happiness and fulfillment, the absence of all desires and aspirations. Living by the truth meant becoming fully aware of every moment and every quiver of the air one breathed, and being able to truly and enthusiastically perceive birdsong as a pageant and a symphony.

Living by the truth meant a celebration of life, the possibility of feeling it in all the pores and components of one's being.

Living by the truth meant the essence of joy that spreads and grows, the kernel of good, for everyone.

A person could only live by the truth if they opened up for it completely, if they constantly reexamined and purified themselves, like a house and its secluded corners are cleaned, and they thus thwarted the building of dark tunnels in their soul, the raising of walls around their own being. No tunnels or walls against anyone have been able to lead a person to the bright glade of the truth.

But the bright purity of the truth could not shine on forever because there were people who lived by the lie, and there were many, many times more of them. People who lived by the lie tried to assure themselves and others that what they lived by was the truth.

If they really lived by the truth they would not need to assure anyone of anything—the light of the truth per se would be sufficient for their peace and fulfillment, even if no one else believed it.

Since they lived by the lie but did not want to admit it to themselves, simply because they were afraid of what would happen if they lived by the truth, afraid of all the things they would have to renounce and all the things they would then have to do without, they needed to prove and demonstrate, constantly and everywhere, that they lived by the truth. Therefore they were constantly offended because they thought inside that someone could doubt they lived by the truth, although they themselves were actually the ones who doubted it most of all.

TATJANA GROMAČA

They were offended and angry, and inside they were always condemning everyone else, which really meant they were always condemning themselves. They were always finding the weak points and faults in others, always criticizing them within themselves, which really meant they were always finding the weak points and faults inside, in themselves, and always criticizing themselves inside.

All that was because they lived by the lie, and they lived by the lie because they were afraid to live by the truth. For fear of encountering the clearing of the truth they were always raising walls within themselves, and that led them to live in lies, because lies are nothing but an accumulation of fears that go unresolved and are considered not to exist.

Every unresolved fear within a person was a big lie and a huge wall, and here there could be no life in the sun, like living by the truth, because the sun could not enter the darkness or between walls. The sun sought total transmittance and openness for its passage—just as a leaf accepts its ray, so too a person absorbs its light with soothing and sublime true joy.

# PART IV

*An attempt to show all the reasons why the dregs*
*of every person are cast up.*

*Speeding up*

THERE WAS NO slowness anywhere anymore, except perhaps in monasteries, temples, and other homes of the spirit, but there was no freedom there either. Everyone everywhere was trying hard to speed up because whoever was speedy and performed their duties so fast that it seemed they would fall apart any minute from the acceleration was efficient, exemplary, and merited that their boss pay them. They just needed to march stiffly as if goose-stepping, hammer away at the keyboard as if they wanted to permanently destroy a letter with each blow, and frantically issue invoices, write out prescriptions, and wield rubber stamps with such vigor that it seemed their arm would drop off at the shoulder.

The world had become a rigidly organized military barracks, within which, to be sure, various undesirables circulated—deserters, drug smugglers, gun runners, and traffickers in human beings and organs—but rules applied in those areas too. Spontaneity vanished at all levels, and the general trend seemed to confirm the predictions of futuristic novels that people would one day become robots. And that day had come. Unnoticed.

The great saving lay in it not being necessary to spend huge amounts on the manufacture of real robots, since humankind showed its adaptability to the general ideal of the robot, which was not only a mechanical person with a stiff body and no soul, and not only as efficient, exact, and effective as the best robot— if it was good, of course—but was also in essence what you get with a robot: a slave.

No one was free, all of them lived by the dictate emitted by ubiquitous large screens, illuminated signs, displays, cameras that followed and filmed everyone, devices that read people's thoughts, TVs and radios, computer and newspaper pages. No one was free, everyone was trapped, even those who did not wish to be. There was no freedom anywhere because each and every brain was diligently washed, from a very early age, by powerful jets. It was all exactly like in Orwell, or maybe a hundred times worse.

*To hate the truth means to love it, and so on*

THERE WERE PEOPLE who were good but did not wish, or maybe did not have the strength, to oppose those in whom evil predominated, and therefore they bent their backs as subordinates and pretended to be happy. Although they thought differently deep inside, the repetition of the words and thoughts of the others gradually made such people change externally and internally, and they became ever more like those who controlled them, whose thoughts became engraved in them after having been pronounced so many times, and it seemed even to them that there were no words and thoughts better or truer.

Without knowing it, they propped up the lies of the world. They were important levers for the maintenance of lies—their prime servants and humble implementers. For love of their masters they hated the truth, which means they actually loved it and yearned for it, but for love of their masters they consented to extinguish even the smallest flame of the truth in themselves. That is how they lived and that is what was demanded of them in the speeches and actions of their masters, who were the personification of the closed passages of love, a love they fervently yearned for and also fervidly hated, or rather loved.

Since families never spoke about fundamental ideas, and emotions—especially beautiful ones—were almost never shown, or only shown with great restraint, as if love, happiness, and contentment were sinful, people chiefly fell ill at a particular stage in life. Their illness served them as a justification for drawing attention to themselves as they searched for a proof of love from those who surrounded them and mostly loved them, except that they never showed it, in line with the general rules of cultured conduct, so in the meantime they had forgotten that it was truly like that.

Such thoughts often came to me on the way to Konzum, the big new supermarket. I used to go there almost every day to train myself in love and composure, like in a fitness studio. It was an especially demanding exercise for me because whenever I went to Konzum something would make my blood boil. Sometimes other shoppers angered me when they pretended not to see people around them. They did not bother to look if anyone was in front of them and if they might knock them with their elbow or basket, and when they did they would not apologize but plowed on like crazy with their shopping as if they were alone in the world.

The saleswomen would anger me because, when serving shoppers, they would always give precedence to glossy ladies in shiny silk jackets with straw-bleached hair and garish bright red rouge on their lips.

Or I got angry because of the stench of the rancid oil, in which the saleswomen of the special "fresh food" department roasted chicken, sausages, and sauerkraut, as well as thick, greasy potatoes and pork cutlets, and they even had the cheek to call it "health food."

Often the stench of the oil, old meat, and sauerkraut in Konzum made me feel nauseous, and being besieged by such circumstances gave me the ideal basis for training myself in love and the overcoming of anxiety, especially if we also take into account that there was no fresh air in Konzum, that the music from the speakers was very loud, and the lighting was too intense, which all together could undoubtedly cause a headache.

Konzum was the ideal arena for training in the most diverse mental disciplines, and if ever it was not enough I would go to Kaufland, which was much bigger than Konzum, and there I could exercise on several training grounds and gym mats simultaneously.

Outings to such menageries gave me the opportunity for reflection and the shifting of most varied thoughts onto my brain's hemispheres, like a tape is rewound from left to right or right to left. It gave me the possibility to rewind and reorder many things so I would always be able to feel I was at the beginning and still had to go through and learn everything, which was largely true.

It was especially good to come back from Konzum or Kaufland with my bags full of shopping and lug them up to the sixth floor because it allowed me to have a good and thorough think about things again, after which I was finally able to just switch off my brain, or rather give my constricted, frightened heart a chance to have its say, which was the whole aim of such training sessions, which ultimately, if I succeeded in my intention, would turn me toward the good and lofty. But I couldn't stay for long on that plinth of sun and light, borne by the daytime currents of my own river of life. New waves came, with new iniquities and difficulties, which I could do nothing more sensible with than note them down in the hope that they would ultimately help me make up my mind, or so I thought, which was self-deception because thoughts recorded in that way actually appealed to responsibility and the obligation to confront them.

*How the Church and priests influence the formation of people's character and the overall development of their personality*

WHEN MOTHER'S PHASE of flying high abated, she underwent another transformation. Now she became something resembling a village fool. She passed the time making pilgrimages to all the houses in the village and spreading the idea of peace and good the way she viewed it herself and the way she experienced it, considering that she kept silent about the truth hidden inside her. And so her idea of peace and good looked like peace and good on the surface, but inside she harbored bitterness, acrimony and pessimism, pugnacity, anger and rage, fatalism and forlornness.

Mother wanted to be a Virgin Mary who wished everyone well, while concealing the desire that the others be stricken by all manner of illnesses and suffering such as befell her throughout her life. She was a messenger pigeon of fidelity and love, but she did not show her own love for other people.

Her gluttony and ambition made her a sanctimonious sermonizer of life's truths, according to which everyone would incur God's punishment. Life was a bitter vale of tears, which everyone had to quietly cry in their corner, and then go forth and spread the ostensible serenity of the feisty and gruff, embittered and offended soul, which never revealed its own weakness to others, and not even to itself.

Like thousands of other religious people who walked the earth in the same way, Mother considered that love of God actually meant subservient devotion and obedience to the calculating sermonizer at church, that dedication to the idea of good actually meant proudly belting out hymns in the choir, and that yearning for eternal life actually meant the avid expectation of impending, sorrowful death and the subsequent obsequies.

All those were Mother's worst traits, but of course she also had a whole number of good ones, in whose light she could shine in the radiance of eternal love. But her fanatical devoutness and devotion to faith and God revealed only her ugly, bad sides, which again it was harsh and a little cruel to accuse her of personally, given her sensitivity and the way she took in the thoughts, states, feelings, and views on life of the people around her. Because ever since she began regularly going to church and attending all the noble prayers, collections, and drives, Mother became a much worse person than before, and for that she certainly ought not to thank her religion and God, at least not God as the eyes of the Church saw Him—the eyes of the Church fathers and the high-minded and charitable church brethren and sisters.

*Marriage as a sacred institution, and divorce as a sin and a catastrophe that must never be allowed to happen to anyone*

THE MAIN IDEA in Mother's life was to spread the ideal of the perfect and consummate marriage in which she lived. It is not completely clear whether that idea was deeply set in her heart as the genuine blossoming of girlhood dreams, or whether it was just the result of deep-seated beliefs and fears she received from her father in childhood, according to which marriage must be kept pure on the outside even at the cost of the greatest inner filth, and marriage was never allowed to be dissolved, not even if it meant ongoing mutual torment, oppression, and enormous suffering of those who had entered into it.

Even in situations when her own marriage felt to her truly, absolutely, and completely hopeless—beyond recovery—it is highly possible that Mother still did not want to admit it to herself by any means, even if it were a matter of life and death, precisely because of the great fear she felt at the very idea of the dissolution of her marriage. So deep and indestructible was her fear of violating the paternal commandments and rules, or so deep was her belief in love.

*Slaves of the dead*

MOTHER WAS A prime example of a person entirely in thrall and not free, shackled by the fears of her ancestors, particularly her father, which goes to prove that it is not significant in the slightest whether the one who has taken control of a person's thoughts and actions is alive or dead, near or far, in touch with them or incommunicado.

A person in thrall can live in complete outward freedom in front of everyone, and yet, most often without knowing it or wanting to admit it to themselves by any means, be in heavy iron chains like in the darkest dungeon, and their jail keepers and masked tormentors can escort them every day, welcome them with the most amiable, amorous greetings, and treat them to a feast of delicious foods and cakes, just like in a fairy tale.

People most often yield to the cheap lures of comfort and amenity, a full stomach and mollycoddling, so conducive to the inertia of the body and soul, because they are weak to temptations whose benefit is very short-lived.

*The shameless minotaur*
*(almost like the dregs in every person)*

SO AT ONE POINT in her life Mother became an animal. She did not strictly "become" an animal because she had always been one, just as every person is an animal deep down in their most hidden and repressed ego, but she wanted to hide and negate her inner animal to such an extent that it broke away from her completely and appeared on the surface as a naked minotaur with a huge erect penis.

Mother's minotaur became tired of hiding. He took out his big, black-bearded member and waved it to and fro, cackling at everyone, taunting and sneering, and belittling everyone he ran into.

Mother's minotaur did everything that was not allowed, and worse. He relieved himself in the middle of the street in sight of people and cars, in front of school children; he was crude, brazen, and ravenous; he devoured piles of fatty foods, piles of sweet and sticky cakes, piles of pastries and breads, piles of cured and cooked meats.

The minotaur wished evil upon everyone: that they fall ill and die so he could go to their funeral, that they all cheat on their husband or wife so they would all be abandoned and disillusioned, that no one love anyone, and that no one sleep with another person in a bed full of passion and sweat.

When Mother was a minotaur she was no good for anyone. She hated herself and everyone else, therefore she did not wash and stank of urine, which everyone called piss, and sometimes she had diarrhea and a huge amount of shit came out of her, which no one could stop.

Once Mother was in the hospital when a lot of shit began to come out of her, but no one wanted to help her wash and change into new clothes. All the women stood against the far wall as if lined up for a firing squad. They watched Mother as she thrashed in pain in her bed full of shit like a tortured, bloody scorpion.

No one wanted to help her. It was so repulsive that everyone was thoroughly disgusted at the idea, but at the same time they wanted to watch Mother's shit and breathe in its stench, because as horrible and disgusting as it was, it was also lovely, unique, and alluring, and so their eyes did not stop absorbing, their nostrils did not stop inhaling, and their ears did not stop listening to Mother's cries for help.

After quite a while, one woman finally came to Mother's aid. She dragged her like a wounded and bleeding soldier to the wall of salvation, which is to say, the bathroom. There, between the black, white, and green tiles, she washed Mother. Then she dressed her in clean, dry clothes, but she immediately wanted to know when, in return, Mother would bring her thirty-five fresh chicken eggs from home.

That was appropriate, in any case, because nothing in this world is free, and helping Mother at that moment in particular was certainly worth much, much more, perhaps as much as a ton of freshly laid eggs, with which someone could make a mass of custards, cream puffs, and whipped cream rolls.

That was when Mother was the minotaur in the hospital. When she was at home and became a minotaur, that meant again that her ego dominated completely and became unbearable for everyone else. Father therefore had to move from the house into his workshop because Mother's ego prevailed completely and dominated all and sundry, such that there was no space or air to breathe for anyone around her anymore.

*It is hard to be in the same room as a minotaur*

FATHER THEREFORE STOKED the stove in the workshop and moved out toward the garden and orchard so that Mother's ego could continue to writhe to and fro until it fatigued and broke. But that did not happen, and ultimately he had to take Mother to see the doctors again because the hospital and white coats were the only things she feared. The doctors had to point at her and threaten to shut her away in a hospital room until the end of her life if she did not calm down and bridle her ego, that is if she did not learn to leave some space for others.

Just when Mother would learn to leave a little space for others, Father's ego would rampage in place of hers and wish everyone to get their just desserts, and suddenly all that had applied until recently no longer did because Mother was now the one who was upright, while Father abruptly went awry, so now he had to be calmed down in order to tame his ego, so it would become concealed and invisible, if it was not possible for it to be eliminated, at least while it was in human shape and form.

*Within all of that, a person falls into a bottomless chasm*

MOTHER BECAME OVERLY strenuous. She imagined she was on the roof of the world. Therefore, from this overreaching vantage point that covered everything, no one was her equal anymore because no one could go so high, except perhaps a general, king, or emperor from the distant past.

But all of them were long since dead, and the arduous task devolved on Mother of shouldering the huge burden of wisdom, greatness, and knowledge, as well as equity, empathy, self-sacrifice, and probably a lot more besides, but not self-examination and self-criticism.

Mother, to that extent, prevailed over everything around her. Her charisma and self-pity were able to win everyone's favor, obedience, and admiration, such that she was able to do exactly what she wished with everyone, a bit like when a child models a toy from clay, or some other pliant material.

Only Father, with whom she shared a roof over her head and a casserole on the table, grasped the full burden of her "greatness and humanism," and that realization left him no choice but to move out of the warm, heated house into the cold, damp workshop in the middle of the courtyard. In doing so, he astonished himself that he had showed his teeth once in a blue moon, in other words he had emphasized that he did not want to be Mother's little clay toy.

An antipathy emerged between Father and Mother, like between the majority of husbands and wives. It had dwelled in their hearts for quite some time, but now it inflated terribly, more and more, like a big balloon the color of human excrement. The more their mutual antipathy grew, the bigger and smellier the pile of excrement between them became.

That went on until the accumulated poison and stench began to make their heads ache. As soon as pain appeared in their bodies, all the accusations and hatred would temporarily stop.

The hatred would not actually disappear but be temporarily repressed and pushed beneath the surface, which now shimmered with pain, sorrow, and self-pity. The only realization that came was that of the fragility and ephemeral nature of the body. They perhaps pondered the soul inside, feared God, and dreaded the divine punishment that was supposed to come, but there was no telling what form it would take and how severe it would be.

*Civilization and its lies—the pharmaceutical industry makes a fortune*

MOTHER STOLE A chocolate bar in the supermarket and also peed in the little park in front of the elementary school, immediately next to the main road and beside the pedestrian and cyclist path where people streamed past. She did these things now, in the years when she should have become a grandmother, because her true age did not correspond to her actual number of years, which were mirrored in her sixty-year-old body.

Mother no longer fit into the system, which required respect for certain rules. These were simple rules of good behavior and etiquette, which for Mother suddenly became hard and impossible to follow.

Prior to civilization, everything was communal, Mother's subconscious thought, including women and men, but with the onset of civilization a woman could no longer belong to multiple men; one man marked her for himself, just as he could thrust a stake into the ground to designate a holding that he considered his from then on. Mother with her new views on the world and her experience of the world belonged to the civilization that predated ours. She wanted to share everything with others and did not care for manners, so she would shout

out to people on the street, laugh loudly in the line at the bank, telephone at six in the morning, and listen to loud music while she cooked at two in the morning. All in all, Mother became a "nutcase," or at least that is how other people saw her.

At the same time, she wanted to control her close friends and family because she was afraid something bad could happen to one of them, or rather because, just like her mother, grandmother, great-grandmother, great-great-grandmother, and all the other medicine women of the Native American tribe Mother was descended from, women whose presence was more like an anti-presence in her life compared to that of the roles men played, she believed deep inside that everyone would suffer a tragic and dreadful event that would crush them once and for all and make them permanently worthy and deserving of others' sympathy and pity, and whose tragedy everyone near and far would tell and tell over again with voices like gloomy chickens with clipped wings during long, leisurely television afternoons and equally idle, even colder, mindless and delirious evenings.

In any case, Mother became what she had always been, only now without shame and concealment, like an über flight controller constantly on duty, checking every day if everyone she knew in any way was alive and well, and in doing so she annoyed everyone because she could never wait for all the people dotted around her to ring and say they were alive and well, but she had to grab the phone at the crack of dawn and call to check if all her relatives, friends, and acquaintances had made it through the dense, black, somber night and lived to see the dawn.

Mother also dug and grubbed through everything in their house to the finest details and deepest depths, from the darkest attic closets and secluded, cobwebbed corners to the dampest basement holes. There was no drawer, box, pen, rag, or toy that Mother's hand did not touch, turn over twice, shake, or

TATJANA GROMAČA

disassemble to see if a miniature bomb, chocolate bonbon, hidden message, or a wad of two hundred euros would drop out.

All this was partly the result of the pills she had been taking for years. Sometimes she downed several handfuls of these psychotropic drugs a day, while other times just half a handful was sufficient for her condition to "stabilize," as the doctors used to say.

Sometimes Mother was so well stabilized that her right arm and left leg constantly shook, and her lower lip trembled and constantly drooped. That was the result of the ever newer and more refined drugs, which prominent professors and doctors gave Mother copiously in order to determine the possible side effects and curative powers of new drugs so that the pharmaceutical industry could expand in the best way possible.

For testing the pills on people, the pharmaceutical industry rewarded prominent professors and doctors with all-expense-paid trips and stays at exclusive hotels with hot tubs somewhere on the Adriatic. Dubrovnik was always an option because it was hard to find anyone immune to the charms of that city, however prominent they were, however high their position, and so perhaps Dubrovnik, or if necessary definitely Dubrovnik and nothing else, could be the magic formula for the full-out propagation and unquestionable effectiveness of a new and astonishingly effective drug regimen.

In any case, the pharmaceutical industry was exceptionally efficient. It could ensure that any person be turned into a deplorable wreck after several years of regularly taking two handfuls of its pills. It could give written confirmation that the drugs would very effectively delete certain emotional regions and certain parts of the personality within that being. It could guarantee long-term and effective stability in the form of the lasting downfall and ruin of its clients, who after ten years of regular consumption of these drugs were no longer fit for life outside of "reservations," but were solely fit for life in "reservations," strictly segregated from the outside world, and where they had to follow the rules of a game that made them obedient patients and semi-slaves, who no longer belonged to the outside world but hovered like little bees from flower to flower, always just having to carry out daily tasks and duties, while obeying the orders of the staff in white there with them behind bars.

*How it was for Mother when I was born,*
*and her use of the expression "as if" again*

"IT WAS SUMMER when you were born, a real heat wave. The sun didn't shine but burned down so hot that people had to shelter beneath the eaves. It was July, the month Miroslav Krleža was born, whose novels I found such a grind to read at school," Mother said.

The day she told me that, I felt her heart was in the right place, as if her heart had just slotted into place in a special way and she was especially lucid at that moment on that day.

"The day you were born, an ambulance came for you and me to drive us to hospital. We didn't have a car the day you were born—we only bought it a year later. So Father had to call an ambulance.

"He had to go down to the river, to the ferry, because the ferrymen had a field telephone. There was no phone anywhere else in the village, so a man whose wife was in labor always went to the ferry to use the phone, and the ambulance came to the ferry to get them.

"Father called me to go with him to the ferry, like other women who had their contractions did with their husbands, but I didn't want to go. I didn't want to be among women who groaned and screamed. They put on airs, acted, and exaggerated with their groaning and screaming, shouting and swearing during their birth pains, a bit like the wailers at funerals.

"Your birth was easy, but with your sister it was much harder. When Ivana came, it wasn't an ambulance that took me to the hospital but our neighbor Branko. To be exact, Father was supposed to drive me in our car when Ivana came, but it was at the garage being repaired. We thought the car would be ready by the time Ivana came . . . as if, but that was a mistake.

"Now it's summer but, believe me, winter will come soon too. The days pass too quickly and time flies. Soon you'll be forty. I'm sixty, and you'll be forty. So we've become closer," Mother said.

This time she did not use "as if," probably because there was nowhere to fit it in. If she had found a place for it she would have tacked it in there because "as if" was a favorite expression of hers. She had not used it for years, but somehow she suddenly remembered it and put it to use again after a long, long time.

TATJANA GROMAČA was born in Sisak, Croatia, in 1971. She studied comparative literature and philosophy at the University of Zagreb. In 2001 she won a scholarship from the Berlin Academy of Arts. From 2000–17 she worked as a journalist for the Split-based *Feral Tribune* and *Novi list* from Rijeka, focusing on culture, the arts, and society. Since 2017 she has been freelancing, writing literary reviews, essays, travel pieces, and contributions on works in the humanities for Croatian radio and online media. *Božanska djećica* (*Divine Child*) earned her the 2012 Vladimir Nazor Prize of the Croatian Ministry of Culture for the best work of prose and *Jutarnji list*'s Novel of the Year prize in 2013. A number of her books have been translated into various languages. She lives in Pula, Croatia.

WILL FIRTH was born in 1965 in Newcastle, Australia. He studied German and Slavic languages in Canberra, Zagreb, and Moscow. Since 1991 he has been living in Berlin, where he works as a translator of literature and the humanities—from Russian, Macedonian, and all variants of the "language with many names," aka Serbo-Croatian. In 2005–07 he translated for the International Criminal Tribunal for the former Yugoslavia. Firth is a member of professional associations in Germany (VdÜ) and Britain (Translators Association). His best-received translations of recent years have been Robert Perišić's *Our Man in Iraq*, Aleksandar Gatalica's *The Great War*, Faruk Šehić's *Quiet Flows the Una*, and Miloš Crnjanski's *A Novel of London*.

willfirth.de

*About Sandorf Passage*

SANDORF PASSAGE publishes work that creates a prismatic perspective on what it means to live in a globalized world. It is a home to writing inspired by both conflict zones and the dangers of complacency. All Sandorf Passage titles share in common how the biggest and most important ideas are best explored in the most personal and intimate of spaces.